The Boy Who Could See Death

The Boy Who Could
See Death

SALLEY VICKERS

VIKING
an imprint of
PENGUIN BOOKS

VIKING

UK | USA | Canada | Ireland | Australia
India | New Zealand | South Africa

Viking is part of the Penguin Random House group of companies
whose addresses can be found at global.penguinrandomhouse.com.

First published 2015
001

Copyright © Salley Vickers, 2015

The moral right of the author has been asserted

A version of 'Vacation' was previously published as a Penguin ebook in 2012

Set in 12.5/14.75pt Garamond MT Std by Palimpsest Book Production Ltd, Falkirk, Stirlingshire
Printed in Great Britain by Clays Ltd, St Ives plc

A CIP catalogue record for this book is available from the British Library

ISBN: 978-0-241-18769-2

www.greenpenguin.co.uk

For the Hosking Houses Trust, with thanks for their
kind hospitality,
And in memory of Deborah Rogers, who loved stories

Contents

Author's Note   ix

The Churchyard   1
Kleptomania   12
The Train That Left When It Was Not
    Supposed To   29
Mown Grass   57
The Boy Who Could See Death   74
Rescue   99
A Sad Tale   113
The Sofa   151
A Christmas Gift   160
Vacation   170

Author's Note

I suppose that behind each story there is always another story. Perhaps this is more likely to be the case with a short story than with a novel, which must be a sort of portmanteau of experiences, whereas a short story usually springs from a single idea or train of thought. People who have read my novels will recognize in this collection some familiar themes: most distinctively, the interplay between life and death, sometimes in a psychological and sometimes in a somewhat supernatural strain. But they may also recognize my preoccupation with place. I have never been able to write about any place that I do not know fairly intimately and I never take my locations on trust from others' accounts. All of these stories have been fostered in some way or other by a particular place, either by my having been there at the time the story occurred to me or through that place having become the locus where a fledgling story idea seemed naturally to settle.

But, reviewing the stories for publication, I was also interested to find that each of them also has some special association with a particular friend, or, in some cases, friends, or member of my family. Again, this is less likely to be the case with a novel, where the scope is naturally wider. But it has pleased me to see how kinship and friendship have often formed the spark that has warmed a latent idea into life.

This collection is dedicated in part to the Hosking Houses Trust, whose generous hospitality I enjoyed while writing several of these stories. The opening story, 'The Churchyard', in particular is informed by my stay at Church Cottage in the little village of Clifford Chambers, close to Stratford-upon-Avon. The physical details of the cottage itself, the churchyard which it overlooks and the white-berried rowan tree growing among the graves may all be seen there by the curious visitor. Even the mistle thrush, with which I became enamoured, may, with luck, still be gracing with its song the rowan outside the bedroom window. And, while I never take any character from life, I did borrow my principal character's Christian name from Sarah Hosking, my kind hostess, who bears a resemblance to Sarah's landlady Clovissa by virtue of her generosity.

Clifford Chambers was also the place where I wrote 'Rescue', which was inspired by the funeral of my dear friend Deborah Rogers, to whom this collection is also dedicated. In no sense is it an account of her funeral except for the fact that that sad event reminded me of the way that death can cause one to see other people, and indeed oneself, with fresh eyes. Deborah was a close friend before I became a writer. We agreed that our friendship was too precious to risk by our becoming professionally involved and for that reason she was never my literary agent. But we spent many, many happy hours together sharing our somewhat forensic and sometimes fantastical view of human nature. I wanted to write a story for her that she, at least, would have relished.

I think Deborah might have also enjoyed 'Kleptomania', since she was a fan of Pekes and eccentrics both. The setting for this story was occasioned by a stay in a house in Dorset that I took one Easter for my family and myself. Happily, our holiday was free from any of the tensions in the story, the only real-life mishap being my somehow managing to make a double order to Waitrose with the result that we were coming down with excess food. We were visited there by a small dog, which my son named Tandoori and with which my elder granddaughter, Rowan, a devotee of all animals but dogs most especially, fell in love. Ho Chi Minh owes something to Tandoori and this story was written for Rowan, who is herself already an accomplished writer.

'A Sad Tale' is also dedicated to Rowan, as she has come to share my love of Shakespeare and was drawn to the fairytale element in *The Winter's Tale* and also to its dark under-themes. The story was conceived when staying with my old psychoanalytic colleague, fellow author and longtime friend, Anthony Stevens, in his house in Corfu. When asked recently by the *Observer* for a choice of summer reading, writers were also asked to divulge their holiday destinations. I, as did the other contributors, obeyed and revealed that I was going as usual to my summer retreat at my friend's lovely old Corfiot farmhouse. For some reason this was considered sufficiently pretentious to appear in *Private Eye*. I've waited years to be in *Private Eye* and could wish it were a funnier entrance but beggars can't be choosers.

Anthony also shares a love of Shakespeare. As a psychoanalyst myself, I'm intrigued by those of Shakespeare's characters who, while central to the plot, lack any substantial physical presence. Or extensive presence. For Mamillius – the boy child who dies in *The Winter's Tale*, and the protagonist in my story – has a crucial dramatic role, curtailed as his appearance is in the play. It is he who, when asked by his mother to tell her a story, gives the play its title, and it is his brief but lambent words that I borrowed for the title of the story I found myself wanting to write about him. I have always baulked at the idea that there is somehow 'redemption' at the close of this play (redemption is a word too glibly bandied about these days); Mamillius, in the play, dies from grief, as a result of his father's insane jealousy, and, unlike his mother and his sister, who are merely believed dead, never returns to us. My story is some attempt to redeem that tragedy by having him develop into a storyteller – and a playwright – himself.

My enthusiasm for children and childhood is well

known among my family (who could sometimes do with less of it) and that has given me a special interest in Shakespeare's children. This story is a relative of 'The Indian Child', which appeared in my last collection, *Aphrodite's Hat*, and its subject was the changeling child in *A Midsummer Night's Dream* and his role in Shakespeare's imagination. It was written for my grandson, Sam, who, as a baby, lay beside me in his carry-cot while I wrote it. It is therefore fitting that 'A Sad Tale' should be dedicated to his beloved cousin Rowan, with whom he has always shared an almost preternatural, indeed Shakespearean, affinity.

'A Christmas Gift' was written in Corfu, though its locus is Venice, scene of my first novel, *Miss Garnet's Angel*. It was once possible to sail from Venice to Corfu, and when I could afford it this was my preferred way of travelling there. (Sadly, no ferry now serves the direct route.) On my mother's side I come from seafarers and perhaps for this reason I am drawn to the sea. I have been privileged to see few sights as sheerly lovely as the view of Corfu approached across the Adriatic at dawn.

'The Train That Left When It Was Not Supposed To' has its footing in Windsor Great Park, which is also the location of Cumberland Lodge, the educational trust for which, at the time of writing, I am a trustee. I am grateful for Cumberland Lodge for many reasons: the excellence of the work it does, the companionship of my colleagues and the good company I have met there over the years. But perhaps I am most grateful for the opportunity to get to know Windsor Great Park. The park is a mysterious and ancient place where it is easy to imagine all kinds of supernatural events occurring. And of course it is the location of one of Shakespeare's funniest plays, *The Merry Wives of Windsor*. The Shakespeare scholar Professor L. C. Knights used to say that there were some scenes in literature that, no matter what, always made him laugh and one was Falstaff hiding in the laundry basket. The anarchy that is in Falstaff's blood seemed to get into the veins of this story.

'Vacation' has its roots in the Western Isles of Scotland, which has some of the most heavenly locations in the British Isles. I have visited many of the Western Isles and I don't know why this location should have brought to mind the idea of a deep and lasting maternal betrayal. As a psychoanalyst, maternal betrayal is not a novel idea to me. And there is something about an island that suggests both abandonment and intensity.

The location of 'The Sofa' is more parochial: Hampstead, and the flat of the parents of an old university friend, Daniel Wolf. After his parents' death my friend took over the flat and, deciding that the old sofa was irreparable, was about to throw it out. I had admired both his parents, Jewish refugees, and their story, and I had a special fondness for his mother, who was kind to me at a time when I was much in need of kindness. For some years I kept the sofa as a tribute to her and the story is its immaterial counterpart. My friend the actor Paul Rhys read it on Radio 4 and his subtle gift for emotional nuance brought out the pathos of a traumatized childhood.

Finally, my title story, 'The Boy Who Could See Death'. This derives from almost a lifetime's interest in death. So far as I can tell, even as a child death never frightened me and as an analyst I worked very often with those who had lost someone close to them or had themselves attempted or nursed a wish for suicide. My oldest friend, another writer, Petrie Harbouri, and I often discuss how helpful it would be to know the hour and date of one's own death. It was she who reminded me of the line in the Order for the Burial of the Dead in the Book of Common Prayer: 'Lord, let me know mine end, and the number of my days: that I may be certified how long I have to live.' Some mixture of these influences must have quickened poor Eli into consciousness. If his life ends in the Welsh Marches, this is because this is another part of the British Isles that has become part of my inner landscape. It was also loved by Deborah Rogers, who, with her husband, the composer, Michael Berkeley, made a home there, which I visited often. Deborah is buried in the sloping grassy graveyard of her little local church at Stowe.

Salley Vickers
2015

The Churchyard

———◄◦►———

When Sarah Palliser looked through the window that morning, the man was standing there. The window wasn't hers. It belonged to the cottage she'd been renting while deciding where, finally, to settle. Quince Cottage (named for a tree allegedly planted for the coronation of Queen Anne) was small, no more than one up and one down if you didn't count the lavatory. But it was tangibly old, and it sided on to a churchyard that could be entered through a door in the high weed-embroidered wall that bound in the garden. From the west face of the church tower a clock magisterially struck the hour. And from the once ancient, now prudently double glazed, windows in the kitchen the stones marking the patient dead could be observed. It was this last that had decided her to take the cottage on a six-month lease.

The dead made good neighbours: unintrusive, incurious. Each morning, when Sarah came down to make her morning tea, she stood looking out at the gravestones while the kettle boiled. One stone in particular she had become strangely attached to. It recalled Charles Blakey of this parish, who had lived thirty-seven years and died in 1836, thus ensuring his short life narrowly spanned the two centuries.

The mornings in the churchyard possessed a soothing similarity. The dead stayed exactly as they were. Few living bodies crossed her line of sight. Only the birds. In all weathers there were birds: blackbirds, the male birds, their yellow bills assertively foremost, hopping with easy familiarity around the gravestones on which robins perched confidently atop; rooks priestly above on the seventeenth-century tower. And the mistle thrush.

The mistle thrush was an especial bonus. On the church side of the cottage's garden wall there grew a rowan tree, that rare enough thing a white rowan, whose berries, against the tawny late November sky, when she had first come, had shone like drops of luminous hail.

It was some time before she had twigged that the mistle thrush's obsession with these berries must be connected to their likeness to those of mistletoe. Though of course the bird was reputed also to eat holly berries, which rather did for that argument. She looked up 'mistletoe' in the dictionary that sat beside Mrs Beeton on the bookshelf. 'Mistle' seemed to derive from 'mizzle', fine mist or rain. The misty origins of the thrush's name appealed to her and had tipped her into approaching Clovissa Jenkins to see if she might consider extending the letting terms from six to twelve months.

Clovissa Jenkins was agreeable, as so far she had been

over most matters. She had obligingly provided, when the weather turned chilly, a hot-water bottle, comfortingly cocooned in pink crochet, and brought round occasional eggs from her hens. The hens, and their imperious rooster ('better than an alarm clock'), had had their part in encouraging Sarah to stay on in Quince Cottage. And of course there was the box.

For she had sworn to herself that she would move nowhere till she had tackled the box.

By the time the year had turned past the vernal equinox and the churchyard was alight with daffodils, Sarah had begun to wonder how she was ever going to leave. For the box remained lurking under the far reaches of the stairs, an invisible but expressive presence of something palpably untackled.

Aside from the perpetual reproach of the box, life in the cottage was simple and sustaining. It was furnished with Edwardian furniture that Clovissa Jenkins had apparently inherited from an aunt. Upstairs was an Arts and Crafts bed with a formidably hard mattress ('such a comfortable bed', Clovissa had assured), a matching chest of drawers, a marble-topped dressing table and a large roll-top cast-iron bath.

The bath stood regally in the bedroom, defying anyone to judge it an unnecessary use of space. On the shelf that ran beside it, Clovissa Jenkins had ranged green glass bottles of an earlier era, and Sarah had provided flowers for one of the several jugs from the workshops of the many esteemed potters with whom her landlady had apparently conducted affairs. She had conveyed this information with a pride that left Sarah uncertain whether it was the number of the affairs or the aesthetic judgement shown by her choice of lovers that fuelled it.

It was after an early bath, when she had gone downstairs in her dressing gown to make tea, that she first saw the man. Or, rather, his feet because the line of the window was only a little higher than the level of the graveyard ground. The brown shoes were standing by Charles Blakey of this parish and, on seeing them, she felt something like indignation. No one, to her knowledge, had approached Charles Blakey since her tenure had begun. She had unconsciously grown proprietorial about his last retiring place. Then, with the freedom that living alone brings (one of its compensations), she laughed aloud at her silliness.

She spent the day wondering whether it was time to open the unbroached box. By 6 p.m. she had contrived to avoid a decision and poured herself a large drink while she watched the news.

The cottage was equipped with both a TV and a DVD player, luxuries that she had been used to doing without since Phillip had disapproved of them. There was something reassuring about the six o'clock news. The violence and prevailing gloom were palliatives to a savaged breast. 'Tomorrow I *will* do it,' she said aloud, pouring another glass of wine. 'Tomorrow I'll be brave.'

The next day she woke to rain and went into Stratford on the pretext of looking at houses. Not any house in particular; more a kind of prowl around to see if she could live there. Stratford had many virtues: the river, the theatre and of course Shakespeare. She and Phillip had rowed about Shakespeare and she had thrown a copy of *The Tempest* at him. 'You're an absurd snob,' she had declared. 'That cloth-eared Earl of Oxford could never have written so sublimely.'

But today Stratford was wet and filled with tourists. If Shakespeare had lived and died there his spirit was sensibly not abroad.

That night the rain cleared and she was wakened by blue moonlight pooling on to the old elm floorboards. It was so bright that it summoned her to sit upright and then pulled her out of bed. Across a sky still ragged with rain clouds the moon was speeding, its lopsided disc conveying a look of manic madness.

A night bird peeped and something moved below. A cat mousing, sliding through the uncut grass. All cats are grey in the dark. If she stood at the window longer she might see an owl. She nursed a hankering for an owl, born of the occasion a barn owl had passed, pale and serene, through the white beam of the car headlights, when she and Phillip still lived together in what she had kidded herself was harmony.

Something else was moving besides the cat. Out of the territory of shadows a shape emerged. A person. A man. And she knew with a shock through her bones that it was the man whose blunt brown shoes she had witnessed the morning before. The interloper on Charles Blakey's grave.

A kind of joyous dread flooded through her. What could he want there alone in the moonlight? As she watched he came towards the cottage and stood as if staring up at her. Could he see her in the uncurtained room?

For some minutes he stood below, a dark pillar in the surrounding darkness, and then he turned away and walked out of sight. For minutes longer she stood looking out of the window while the moon continued its endless race through the torn clouds.

She slept fitfully but near morning fell into a sleep so deep that it was after nine when she descended the stairs for her tea. She was almost afraid to look through the window, unsure whether or not she wanted to see him there again. But only the memory of Charles Blakey faced her stonily.

Later that morning, braced by three cups of coffee, she peeled brown tape back from the box and extracted a clutch of long white envelopes.

'Darling Girl,' began the first letter written in Phillip's distinctive black hand. 'I miss you as I would miss the blood from my veins.'

Squatting on the floor she read on. 'When I was a boy,

walking to school down the country lanes, I would imagine all the little hedge creatures my special friends. That is how I see you – shy and retiring, known truly to no one but me.'

It was terrible how nauseatingly this read now, when once it had thrilled her. Punishing herself, she read more. 'Darling creature, I shall only treat you with the gentleness your loving timid nature deserves –'

Sentimental garbage written by a man who had dumped her only two years after writing it, two years during which, progressively, she had felt as if her skin were being peeled back layer by layer. But of course, all sentimentalists are sadists. She knew that; had always known it. Suddenly, unnervingly, she began to cry.

The box was full of hundreds of such communications, letters, notes, cards she had faithfully, insanely, stored away. Desperately she opened another long white envelope.

'Beloved Sah, what would I do without you?'

Clearly very well was the short answer to this. Should she torch the whole horrible collection and thus put it out of her mind, which it wouldn't? Or should she make herself read his filthy fickle words and cure herself by despising him into oblivion? Putting on her boots, she left the cottage with wet cheeks and walked determinedly down the lane to the river.

A heron stood staring aloofly into the water. She was past wanting to throw herself in but how convenient to be a bird without a heart to be broken. Not broken, she corrected. Paltered with. Worse than broken.

Back at the cottage the open box greeted her balefully. Picking it up, she carried it outside to the garden, where a shed housed a washing machine and a tumble dryer, no longer functioning. 'You can stay there, pig face,' she said and kicked the box hard.

The moonlight didn't waken her that night but towards dawn she was roused by a cry outside. Perhaps an animal in its death throes caught by the churchyard cat? The clock on the church had chimed. Light was pearling hazily through the window, and she got up more for the pleasure of watching the coming dawn than to check the time.

And there he was. Standing, quite visibly this time, by Charles Blakey, with his head bowed as if paying his respects.

Very quietly Sarah opened the window. The man didn't look up, and she heard that he was weeping. Harsh raw sobs. Deeply shocking. Instinctively she called out, 'Please don't cry.'

He looked up then and she had an image of a white face and dark hair and dark, dark eyes. For a long moment he held her in his gaze before she turned and ran downstairs. But when she reached the kitchen window to look again he had gone.

*

8

The following morning, when Clovissa Jenkins was passing, Sarah asked if there were anywhere she might make a bonfire.

'Not in the garden, please. It's far too small.' For once her landlady sounded sharp.

'Oh, no,' Sarah hurried to reassure. 'I wondered if at the end of your garden, maybe.' She had seen an old dustbin there that looked as if it served as an incinerator.

'If you give me whatever it is, I'll see to it.'

But of course she couldn't do that. The box would have to stay in the shed until she found some means to dispose of it.

But its presence pricked her attention viciously so that she couldn't settle. She set off in her car to tour the nearby villages, pretending to be on a mission to find a suitable place to move. But it was hopeless. Until she had dealt with Phillip she would never be able to contemplate being settled. And soon she would have to look for a job. The money he had tossed at her was running out. Frugal as she'd been, she would have to earn a living again soon.

By the time she got back to the cottage she was worn to a ravelling and only a bath in the regal tub offered remedy. Well soaked and wrapped in a towel, she opened a bottle of wine, determined to get soaked in that other sense. She had missed the TV news so she turned on the radio. But as she adjusted the dial she heard a noise outside.

Opening the front door, she saw the shed door was

ajar. A wave of anger engulfed her. Clovissa. No doubt seeking to 'help' by removing her papers. Oblivious to the towel, which was all that covered her, she stormed into the shed.

The man was bending over the box.

'Shall I take these?' His voice had a quiet country burr.

'Why not?' she found herself saying. It seemed so easy to let him.

'Better they're gone.'

She wondered if she should ask him in for a drink – but that seemed somehow impertinent. 'Is there anything –' she began to ask but he forestalled her.

'Nothing,' he said, and looked at her as if he were someone who had known her, loved her even. 'Nothing more to be done now.'

She saw he was looking towards the door that led from the garden into the churchyard and she went to open it. 'Shall I see you again?' she couldn't help asking.

'Perhaps.'

'Perhaps?'

'Oh, it depends.' His smile was gently respectful.

Looking after him through the open door, she saw nothing more than Charles Blakey's solitary stone.

The next morning two men were there. Loud men, smoking and laughing, with diggers. How dare they. How dare they molest his resting place. Opening the door to the churchyard, still in her dressing gown, she shouted, 'What are you doing?'

'Only their business.' It was her landlady with eggs. 'The Blakey family is burying their son.'

'Charles Blakey of this parish?'

'His great-great-grandchild. Quite a young man but his wife had left him, apparently, and one doesn't like to speculate but the means of death hasn't been . . .' Too well bred to spell out the regrettable, her landlady faded into silence.

'What was his name?'

'Peter. No, Phillip. Yes, Phillip. Not an attractive name but then I'm so lucky with mine.'

Sarah watched the funeral from the kitchen window. When the last of the mourners left she saw that the mistle thrush had returned to the rowan and was busily devouring the last few mizzle drops of berries.

Kleptomania

——◄○►——

(for Rowan)

Having Cousin Francesca to stay was a mixed blessing. Not that she was exactly a cousin – rather, one of those offspring of some past cousin whose precise relationship it was always hard to fathom, if, indeed, it was ever rightly known. The best that could be said was that at some point, sometime, some members of the family had been cousins and Cousin Francesca was a surviving twig off this branch.

Some version of the above was coursing through Peter Verney's mind as he walked through Mulberry House (where his family traditionally spent Easter) removing the obviously portable items, all very familiar to him after so many years of staying there. For whatever blessings issued from Francesca, her propensity to pilfer was not one of them. Kleptomania his wife, Kay, called it.

But Francesca, whatever her precise relation to him, was blood, which was said to be thicker than water (if not obviously the better for that), and in Peter's view kleptomania was too harsh a verdict – more a characteristic eccentricity, he would call it, as she rarely took anything of value – though, as Kay had remarked, a medical diagnosis had the virtue of removing any suggestion of moral turpitude. Kay, not unreasonably, was less indulgent of his relative's failings. On the other hand, his wife was fair-minded, one of the several reasons for marrying her, and admitted that Francesca was wonderful with the children.

The children, of whom there were five (Peter liked to say that, while they had 'practised' contraception, they had never quite got the hang of it, a 'witticism' which made Kay wince), found no admixture in the blessings of Cousin Francesca. They referred to her uninhibitedly as 'Fran' and looked forward to her visits with an enthusiasm that might have made a less fair-minded mother jealous. It had long been established that Fran would sleep in the attic alongside the three girls.

The four beds were ranged as in an army-hospital ward, and even resembled something military in being made of iron. The boys, James and Tobias, as the eldest and youngest respectively of the Verney family, had individual rooms. The girls, Judith, Clara and Winifred, had all arrived barely a year apart; almost indecently close together. This had resulted in their being brought up pretty much as triplets, which had produced what could be a formidable group personality.

The boys, as is often the way, were made of less stern stuff. James, the elder boy, had a stammer, which no one could attribute to any emotional mismanagement by his parents and of which he seemed to be almost proud. Francesca, in fact, had had more than a minor role in James's way of taking on an apparent impediment, having pointed out to him, when he was still very young, that a stammer was ripe to be exploited. People, she counselled her young nephew, were nervous of stammerers, and James might usefully consider the bar as a profession when the time for such decisions came.

Tobias had nothing to exploit other than his undeniably red hair. The hair was also the subject of his father's heavy humour. There was no red hair in either side of the family, and Peter liked to refer to a red-headed mechanic who had mended the family car around the time of Tobias's birth. Many people found this joke embarrassing, because they were unsure how much truth there might be in it, which added to Peter's amusement and to his wife's irritation.

Cousin Francesca arrived later that day with a number of brilliantly coloured scarves wound about her neck, a straw sunhat, with a green-feathered budgie enlivening its brim, and a live Pekinese with a blue-spangled collar and a crimson lead.

The Peke had not been expected. Indeed, its existence was news to the Verneys and the children swooped on it with delight.

'Can she stay in our room?' the youngest girl, Winifred, pleaded.

'Freddie, darling, no pets, you know the house rules.'

'But that's not fair. You said Toby could have his snake!'

'It's not a snake, it's a slow worm,' Tobias protested. 'And they're an endangered species.'

'Worm, then. But please, Daddy, please, she's only little.'

'Actually,' Cousin Francesca corrected, 'Ho Chi Minh is a boy.' Among Francesca's more annoying affectations, in Peter's view, was her posture of ardent socialist.

'Please, please, *please*, Daddy, can't Ho Chi Minh sleep in our room?' This time it was Judith, known to be her father's pet. The other two girls didn't mind this too much, as Judith could often wangle benefits to suit them all. But on this occasion the plea was fruitless.

'No, he can't. You know how fussy Mrs Bramling is about pets. Ho Chi Minh will have to sleep in the woodshed.'

'Over my dead body,' Cousin Francesca pronounced. 'Ho Chi Minh is highly strung.'

'Oh, Daddy, look he's hurt. You've hurt him.'

The dog was staring up at Peter with bulging brown marble eyes.

'He will sleep in his basket, as usual, beside me.' Cousin Francesca indicated a round shopping basket of the sort found in the illustrations to old-fashioned children's books.

Kay raised her eyes to heaven, recognizing defeat in

her husband's 'Well, on your head be it, Francesca, if we are forbidden to come here again.'

As Peter was later to say, 'The holiday was all right as holidays go, and, as holidays go, it went', a line borrowed without Peter comprehending its point from a satirist introduced to him, as it happened, by Cousin Francesca. Perhaps that in itself was an ominous sign. Nothing especially untoward occurred during her stay. Francesca spent quite a bit of time down the lane with Mrs Bramling, who didn't get about as much as she used to on account of her legs, comparing methods of pickling and the medicinal powers of herbs. Ho Chi Minh achieved added glory with the children by seeing off Mrs Bramling's big tomcat, Angus, who had been staking out a family of young robins being raised in the woodshed.

The weather was unseasonably hot. Extra supplies of beer and water were ordered in from the Dorchester Waitrose, and Cousin Francesca, flirting outrageously with the deliveryman, was overheard asking him back to 'partake of some of the beer one evening'. The children waited for some hours on the wall at the end of the lane, where she had made the appointment to meet, and were bitterly disappointed when he didn't turn up. 'We hoped you'd marry him, Fran,' Winifred lamented.

'Not my type, Freddie. I never like a man with dyed hair.'

'But why did you ask him, then? Why did you ask him to "partake"? What is "partake"?'

'The fun of it, Fred. You'll find out one day. To tell you the truth, I knew he wouldn't come. He'd a swocking great ring on his left hand. I never care for that in a man either.'

'But what does "partake" mean?'

'I didn't want you to marry him,' Tobias said. 'He had hair coming down his nose. Loads of it.'

'Ugh, how uncool,' was Judith's verdict and it was generally agreed that 'partake' was a silly word and Fran must on no account marry anyone with nasal hair.

The baby robins emerged unscathed and were accordingly named Freckles, Clown Mouth, Red Admiral, Fluffy and Norman. ('Why "Norman", Freddie?' 'He's my bestest friend at school and his feathers look like Norm's hair after PE.' 'He isn't really Norman,' Clara confided. 'But he doesn't like his real name.') Supervised by their fretting parents, the robin siblings tottered and swayed gingerly on the snowy branches of the blossoming blackthorn. Under Cousin Francesca's instruction, and rewarded generously with custard creams, Ho Chi Minh was taught by the children to jump through a hoop and, also under her generalship, they organized a ceremonial burial of their father in the sands of Weymouth. During the entombment his new sunglasses were first mislaid and then found to be irreparably broken. This relatively minor mishap was followed by Tobias floating out to sea on a blow-up crocodile that Francesca, behind their parents' backs, had bought for the children.

Kay, when this act of disloyalty was discovered, had attempted to get Francesca to return this to the beach shop where she had bought it but was thwarted by the children, who had already blown it up with a pump lent to them by the man hiring out deck chairs.

('What about him, Fran? He hasn't got any nasal hair.'

'He hasn't got any hair on his head either. Or not enough. I'm not on for bald men.')

Happily, Toby was rescued by an elderly gay couple in a pedalo and towed back to shore, where he was heartily congratulated by his siblings.

'Well done, Tobe, we thought you were off for F-F-France.' James, who could feel outnumbered by the girls, was proud that his little brother was keeping up the male side.

Toby, who had been scared by his adventure, became cocky. 'I would've done if those men hadn't catched me.'

Tobias was heartily scolded by his mother, who also scolded her husband for attempting a joke about pedalos and paedophiles. ('Very feeble but also offensive, Peter. You can't say things like that these days, for God's sake.') This, while assuredly deserved, was really in lieu of scolding Cousin Francesca, who was chatting roguishly with the rescuers.

('Fran,' Clara whispering, 'you can't marry either of them. They're married to each other.'

'I know. A pity. I quite fancy the tall, skinny one with the neat beard.'

'You said you didn't like beards when we suggested the puppet man. Are we going to see them? Only Mummy never lets us see Punch because he's violent.'

'It depends on the beard, Clara. You'll find out. Don't worry. I'll give your parents the money for the puppet show.'

The only other regrettable event was Cousin Francesca's all-round purchase of candy-floss. Kay, who was keen on health foods, had already relaxed sufficiently, in her eyes, by allowing fish and chips for lunch. To have this followed by a gross sugar excess was clear treachery on her husband's relative's part.

'She'll be gone tomorrow and anyway we always had candy-floss as kids and –'

'It never did you any harm? Only rotten teeth and a pot belly.'

'Hey, steady on!' Peter, unhardened to such attacks from a usually tolerant wife, was hurt.

'Sorry, but she's such a shit stirrer. She knows I don't approve of Punch and Judy, and she's gone and told the children that we'll take them to it when she's gone.'

'Why didn't she take them herself?'

'Oh, I don't know. Some nonsense about a beard, Freddie says. To be honest I didn't really listen. It was obviously Francesca being fanciful.'

'It's just her way of having fun.'

'It's just her way of being perverse, you mean.'

Peter sighed. He tended to sigh during Francesca's

visits. 'I know. But she does love the kids and tomorrow she'll be gone and it'll just be us. Can you hang on, darling?'

Kay was mostly a rational woman and she gamely hung on and waved Cousin Francesca off with smiles and fickle promises to enjoy the Punch and Judy.

'Thank God,' she said, collapsing dramatically on to Mrs Bramling's chintz-covered Chesterfield.

'Why are you saying "Thank God"?' Winifred asked.

'Mummy's just pleased to have you to ourselves, Freddie,' Peter suggested.

'We like it *so so so* much better when Fran's here,' was the ungrateful response.

And, indeed, the children played less harmoniously and declared themselves more often bored in the absence of their large playmate. Judith announced she was too old to play with her sisters now, Winifred broke Tobias's walk-down-the-wall Spiderman, which, as he indignantly protested, he'd bought with his own money, James developed a nasty sty on his eye, and Clara found Fluffy dead and impaled on a blackthorn twig and became inconsolable.

'It's 'cos Ho Chi Minh wasn't here to defend her.'

'But how do you know it's Fluffy, darling? It could be one of the others.'

'Oh, great, Mum. So are you saying it wouldn't matter if Red Admiral had d-d-died?'

'Of course not, James. It's just that baby robins look very much alike.'

'I *know* it's Fluffy. Fluffy was my robin.' Clara, red-faced, was furious. 'Are you saying you wouldn't know me if it was me dead?'

'Mum'd probably be relieved if it was you dead, cry baby.'

'Mummy!'

'James! That was horrible. Don't hit him, Clara, darling. Hitting never did any good.'

'In the olden days he would have been whipped on his bare bottom and sent to bed without his supper,' Clara said. 'And Fran would've been our nurse and looked after us properly. I wish she was here with Ho Chi Minh, and you and Daddy had gone to Majorca like Daddy said he wanted.'

'Darling, that was just Daddy being funny.'

'It wasn't funny. You said it wasn't. You said, "Shhh, Peter, the children might hear you," and we did.'

On the day of their departure, the cases packed, the sand shaken from shoes and duly swept from the kitchen floor ('because we don't want Mrs Bramling's help complaining about the mess we left behind') and under the carpet in the hall (because 'she won't notice it there'), Peter began to replace the portable ornaments.

'Kay, you haven't seen the fox, have you?'

'What fox?' Kay was on her stomach fishing out a sock from under James's bed. 'Heavens, James, I think this must be one you left last year. It's positively stiff.'

'You know, the little silver fox which always sits on

the coffee table in the sitting room. I tidied it away from Francesca.'

'Perhaps she took it.'

'She can't have done. I hid any last thing she could pocket before she came.'

'Maybe she found your hoard.'

'I locked everything in my suitcase.'

'Anyone can open your suitcase when it's locked, Daddy,' Judith said. 'It's simple. You just use a fork.'

'What?'

'We did it when you confiscated our Easter eggs when we had that fight. You didn't notice?'

'No. I did not. That's appalling. I suppose Cousin Francesca put you up to that?'

'Kind of.'

'That means she's only gone and bloody well nicked a very valuable item while you were stuffing your greedy little faces with chocolate. You realize that's done it as far as Mrs Bramling goes. I happen to know that fox was given her by her husband.'

This, one of those lies invented to make the hearer feel worse about a situation, was water off a duck's back to Judith. 'He's been dead for ever.'

'That's hardly the point, Judith. And very callous of you, by the way. If I died, don't you think Mummy would want to keep the things I'd given her?'

'She might want to sell them.'

'Judith!'

'Well, she might. What would it matter if you were dead?'

'Judith!'

'I would never sell anything that Daddy gave me,' Kay soothingly interposed.

'So why's the thingy over here, then, if it's so precious?'

'It's a fox. Not a "thingy". And it isn't over here, that's the point.'

'Daddy, you're not being rational.'

Hearing his own frequently repeated words to his children mirrored back at him, Peter finally lost his rag. 'For Christ's fucking sake, if she thinks we nick her things she'll never let us stay here again.'

Kay said, 'Peter! Really!'

Judith stuck her tongue out at her father and the two younger girls began to chant, 'Daddy said the "f" word. Daddy said the "f" word.' Laughing hysterically, they rolled about the sofa until Clara fell off and hit her head on the edge of the coffee table and began to cry.

'Calm down, girls, Daddy's just a bit worked up.'

Freddie began to chant, 'Daddy's got his knickers in a knot.'

'I don't wear knickers,' Peter snapped.

'Daddy doesn't wear knickers. Daddy doesn't wear knickers,' Clara joined in. 'Have you got a bare bum, Daddy?'

Kay said, 'Stop it, girls. And don't say "bum", please.'

'Why not? Fran says it's in Shakespeare. And she isn't lying 'cos she showed us.'

'Girls, you're being complete pests. Darling, let's ring her and find out.'

'Who? Mrs Bramling?'

'No, Francesca.'

'She's not going to admit to anything. Cow.'

Kay mouthed 'Peter!' Too late. Clara and Freddie began to moo loudly.

'She might if we tell her what hangs on it. Let me do it. You're in a state.'

'We wondered,' Kay suggested, 'if maybe Ho Chi Minh had found it in Peter's suitcase and taken it into his basket?' But tact fell on stony ground. Cousin Francesca was icy and resolute. Ho Chi Minh would not be interested in silver. Nor had she any recollection of the ornament.

'The thing is, Francesca' – Peter, who had taken over the phone, was annoyed to hear his voice sounding wheedling – 'if we don't find it I doubt we'll be allowed back.'

'What I can't understand, Peter,' was the response, 'is what it was doing in your suitcase in the first place.'

'It's a fair point,' Kay said. 'If you'd not cleared it away it might have been here still.'

Sometimes there were few things more maddening than a fair-minded woman. 'That's *so* helpful, Kay. What am I going to tell old Ma Bramling?'

'I don't know. Say it vanished. Say the cat got it.'

'We don't have a cat. There was the dog. Perhaps we can suggest that wretched little Peke ate it.'

'I thought you said she wouldn't allow a dog here.' This was Judith again. 'You said we weren't to say. You said –'

'Shut up, Judith.'

'You keep telling us to shut up. If we did that, you'd say we were being rude.'

'Oh, go and play.'

'I don't play any more,' Judith said. 'Playing's boring.'

'Kay, I don't s'pose we could find another?'

'Is that possible?'

'We'd better try.'

After further consultation with Kay, Peter rang Mrs Bramling and asked if they might stay on for a couple of days if no one else was coming to the cottage. Seemingly no one was – the children were delighted, and Peter and Kay set about a thorough-going search among the antique shops of west Dorset, while the children, untended, raided the biscuit tin, ate the crisps and Kit-Kats, and read the comics slipped to them by Cousin Francesca as parting offerings.

Energetic inquiry produced all manner of silver creatures: hares, hens, dogs, ducks, rabbits, otters, even a silver crab which Kay said she was tempted to buy for herself. But not a fox in sight.

'Does it mean we'll never be allowed to come here

again?' Winifred wailed after her parents' day trudging the antique shops had yielded nothing.

'Shut up, Freddie. Yes, I expect it does and it's all your fault, you children, for being greedy.'

'Your fault for locking away our eggs,' was James's riposte.

'You shut up too, James, or I'll wallop you.'

'You can't. It's illegal. I could get the p-p-police.'

'Mum,' Judith said, 'you'd better come. Freddie's stuck a berry up her nose. We've tried to get it out but it's stuck and Toby says she'll have to go to hospital and she's scared.'

'Tell her not to be so silly and to blow her nose hard. It's me as'll end up in hospital at this rate.'

'Are you having a nervous breakdown?' Judith asked hopefully. She could already see herself acquiring kudos with this exciting news at school.

'Don't be absurd, Judith. I've got a monstrous headache and the paracetamol's packed away somewhere.'

But very late on the last afternoon they struck lucky. A little silver fox, miraculously like the missing one, was located in a shop in Dorchester. The owner, observing the eager relief on Peter's face, mentally bumped up the price by twenty pounds.

'That's ninety-five pounds, sir.'

'Really? The hare we didn't buy was only fifty.'

'That's hares. There's more of them made than foxes. Silver's pricey nowadays and it's a lovely little model.'

'Can he be right about hares?' Peter asked in the car. 'I would have thought hares were rarer.'

'Oh, what does it matter if we've found the bloody animal? Now at least we can go home. I'm frankly exhausted. This was meant to be a holiday.'

'It's not a bad resemblance, is it?' Peter asked his wife. The fox had resumed its position on the coffee table beside *The Life of the Weasel* and the *Homes & Gardens* magazines of 1998, and they were preparing to leave at last. 'I mean, she can't have looked closely at it for years. Any small differences won't be noticed, d'you think?'

'I don't know,' Kay said. 'To be frank it's just always been there on the coffee table when we've come. I've never examined it closely. I rather agree with Judith. If it's so hugely valuable, what's it doing in her rented cottage?'

'Well, you know she makes a thing about only taking special clients. Let's hope for the best. But I'm going to say this now: Francesca is never coming away with us again.'

'Daddy!' The two smaller girls began to cry noisily.

'You're mean,' Tobias said.

'You're a tyrant,' was Judith's verdict. 'Worse than Peter the Great. Much worse,' she added darkly. 'At least Peter the Great didn't pretend to be a loving father.'

Two days after the family returned home to London, Peter received a letter.

Thank you so much for the gift of the little fox. There was really no need. Fond as I was of the other one, I sold it to a nice man who runs an antique shop in Dorchester along with a few other trinkets. With Time's winged chariot on the horizon I'm trying to clear the decks a little in readiness for the Great Adventure. But since you've been so kind as to give me this one I shall put it in my own house and treasure it.

Kindest Regards,
May Bramling
PS Please tell your delightful cousin that it is tansy I was trying to remember for worming the dear little doggy. Such a poppet.
PPS I have invoiced you for the three extra days, as requested.

The Train That Left When It Was Not Supposed To

———◄◉►———

Is anything sadder than a train
That leaves when it's supposed to . . .?
– Primo Levi

The first sign that something was amiss was the train that left when it was not supposed to. The would-be passengers were standing – variously eager, impatient, bored or resentful – beneath the illuminated 'Departures' notices at King's Cross. Quite clearly, the sign for the train to York read 11.25 ON TIME. No notice was given of the platform number. And then, at 11.12 a.m. precisely, with no further notice, the board in rapid succession read NOW BOARDING and then almost immediately TRAIN DEPARTED.

Two other odd things happened that day. The visitors to Stonehenge, who had queued patiently to see the ancient stone circle, were attacked by a swarm of apparently violently angry bees, and several people with allergic reactions to the stings were hospitalized. And there was more than one report of a creature resembling a wolf sighted in Windsor Great Park.

'But there've been no wolves in England since Tudor times,' Nan Maitland observed as her husband turned off the TV.

'Well, it's sheer nonsense of course.' Matthew Maitland was a scientist. He loved his wife but had never come to terms with her readiness to be beguiled by the weird or strange.

'Do you think it escaped from a zoo?'

'If it exists.' Her husband had already left her realm of speculation and was reabsorbed in a paper he was refereeing for *Nature* concerning the ethics of animal experimentation.

Nan was an artist. When she met Matt she was working as a waitress in a modest restaurant, more of a glamorized snack bar, really, near the Medical Research Council where Matt held a position at the time. He had taken the then Minister for Science and Education to the restaurant in order, as he later confided to Nan, 'to take the arsehole down a peg'. Nan had spilled water on the arsehole's trousers, causing embarrassment to the Minister and mirth to Matt, who had left so large a tip that she had thanked him the next time he came to the restaurant to eat alone. He had asked her out to eat in a definitely superior restaurant near his flat in Camden Town and at the end of the evening asked if she would like to come back to his place for coffee. It was maybe the only time they had really understood each other.

But good marriages are not always based on mutual understanding. Matt had gone on to head a major clinical research unit near Swindon, and Nan had been able to abandon waitressing and simply paint. This, it turned out, she had a talent for. A gallery in Windsor courted her and she found an aesthetically dilapidated house with a perfect garden with a shed at the bottom, which she converted into a studio.

The studio was not a refuge exactly. But it was her space, with an atmosphere distinct from the main house, with its own kitchen, bathroom and telephone and an array of objects that would have provoked questions from Matt. Perfectly benign questions; but any question has the potential to be felt as an irritant or goad. Stumps of wood, rolls of wire, a rusty part of a plough, a rudder, a balding toy horse on wheels, of the kind that children learn to walk with, would have provoked queries that she didn't want to deal with. Often there are no answers to other people's questions.

There had been nights – not too many – when she had stayed in the studio, when Matt was ill, for example, or his sister Genevieve was staying, or they, she and Matt, not Matt and Genevieve, who were unnaturally polite to each other, were in the throes of a quarrel. But they didn't quarrel often. Maybe not often enough.

Matt was a man of habit. He left the house early and came home and worked. Very occasionally, they went out to dinner and even more occasionally drove in to London, to the theatre or a concert. Mostly, they let each other alone, which is the unsung secret of a good deal of human happiness, except in bed, where the only shadow over their ardour was the absence of children.

'Do you mind?' Nan had asked this only twice, a testament to her considerable self-control.

The truth was that Matt didn't mind. He liked not to be bothered too much so he could concentrate on work and he was clear-sighted enough to know that children are bothersome. Of course it was she who was the one who 'minded'.

Nan had chosen the house in Windsor because of its proximity to the gallery, but she had quickly discovered the charm of Windsor Great Park. Her speciality was painting light and light was a speciality of the park, which has retained, with its ancient royal protection, something of royalty's ancient ambience. Nan walked there daily with her sketchbook, but now she walked looking for the wolf.

'Wasn't there some book?' Matt asked a few nights later. *Women Who Run with the Wolves.* I hope you're not becoming one of those.'

'I might.' Nan was reading *A Short History of the Wolf in Britain.* 'I might in actuality be a werewolf and lope off at night and worry the royal deer.'

'Aren't werewolves always men?' Matt suggested.

'That was then. Times have changed.' She grinned

at him, showing off her admittedly beautiful canine teeth.

Public speculation about the rebellious train was kept to a minimum at the behest of the newly appointed Minister for Roads and Rail while the authorities pursued their inquiries. But the mystery only deepened. It was established that there had been no passengers aboard, but at first it seemed obvious that the train driver must have been in position. Then there was speculation that the man who ran the buffet car and the girl who managed the buffet trolley may have been in place. Matters became more worrying when it was discovered that both driver and guard had called in sick, leaving, in human terms, only the buffet staff unaccounted for. The investigation naturally turned to the question of a hijack but nothing sinister was reported and nothing untoward showed up on any CCTV footage.

Suspicion now centred on the buffet staff, Melvyn Sparks and Monika Cackowski, clearly no relation, though a clandestine attachment was mooted, fuelled by the very human desire to add romance to any mystery.

'That's odd,' Nan said, when she read the names in the *Guardian* (which was running this story as a comment on the mounting failure of the current government). 'I know that name.'

'What name?'

'Monika Cackowski. I'm trying to think how I know her.'

'Probably a very common name in Poland.'

But Nan didn't think that was the explanation.

It was while she was walking in the park, eyes sharpened in hope of a wolf sighting, that the association with Monika Cackowski came back to her.

It was at the gallery. A man had come in and bought one of her paintings. She had been there bringing some canvases for her next show, and the man had seen them and recognized them as by the artist a sample of whose work he was engaged in buying at the time. He left his card with the gallery manager, and when Nan had asked if she could see it, the name Monika Cackowski – she was almost sure it was that – was handwritten on the back. The name printed on the card was so ordinary she hadn't retained it. Peter someone or other, so far as she could recall, and an address in Primrose Hill.

Nan always left her mobile in the car when she walked in the park, so it wasn't till she was driving home that she rang the gallery, breaking the law as she did so. ('There are so many nannying laws these days it seems almost a moral necessity to break them,' she had complained recently to Matt.)

'Austin, have you got the name of that man who bought one of my August Dawns?'

'The one who was interested in the November Night?'

'Him.'

'Half a mo. It's – oh frack it where did I put it?' Austin,

a keen environmentalist, was attempting to introduce a new 'f' word.

'Can you ring me back when you find it?"

Nan returned to the studio and the seventh of the November Night canvases, the series she was engaged in painting. For this one, she was working in greys and whites with varying degrees of brown and black. Black was notoriously tricky. Only Manet really managed it well but it was good to experiment. She settled into the far right corner of the canvas, where the murk was gathering thickly. As she painted she found a shape seemed to be emerging. The phone rang.

'Peter Randall.'

'What?'

'Sorry. Peter Randall's the name of your latest fan.'

'Thanks, Austin. Does he have an email?'

'Half a mo. Yep. prandall@shieldwolf.com.'

'Shield Wolf?'

'Yep.'

'Thanks, Austin.'

'You're welcome.' Austin knew that she loathed that phrase.

'Back to the drawing board, I s'pose.'

'Have a nice day.'

'Austin, stop it!'

'You're welcome.'

Smiling as she returned to her canvas, for she was half in love with Austin for his ability to perceive what irked her (a knack that Matt had never troubled to acquire), she observed that the swathe of brown and grey in the right-hand corner had resolved into a distinct form. A creature. A creature with glaring eyes. Beyond question, a wolf was now skulking top right of *November Night 7*.

Nan looked at her palette. White was there but there was no sign of any yellow. And yet there were the two tiny spots of cadmium yellow and white on the canvas to contradict her. The evidence of her own eyes. She put the brush back down and went to make a pot of coffee.

While the kettle was boiling, she Googled Shield Wolf. No company came up, but a long way down the list of wolves and shields she found 'Randall – Old English for Shield Wolf'. Could this possibly be just a coincidence?

'Darling,' Matt had said one day, 'a universe without coincidence would be very abnormal. Statistically there has to be a fair percentage of coincidences. It's nothing mystical, I'm afraid.'

He wasn't 'afraid' at all. But anyway this was surely more than coincidence. A wolf in Windsor Great Park, a man whose name meant wolf buying a painting which was part of a series in which a wolf had weirdly emerged – though, wait a bit, he hadn't bought *November Night 2* or *3*, only admired them. Most likely, then, it was her unconscious creating the *November Night 7* wolf, though how the yellow had got into the painting beggared belief. She used yellow sparingly.

The kettle boiled and she tipped water into the cafetière and stirred the coffee. Waiting for it to brew, she returned to her laptop and wrote an email, went back to the coffee, poured herself a cup, heated milk in the microwave and returned to the laptop.

Dear Mr Randall,

We met briefly in the Windsor gallery, where you had kindly bought one of my paintings. Might you like to come to my studio to see some more of my work? I am just finishing one in the series part of which I showed you.

Best Wishes
Nan Maitland

There couldn't be much harm in sending it. She knew that Matt would advise her against an invitation to a stranger. But Matt was often needlessly cautious. She hesitated, looking across to *November Night 7*. The lupine eyes glinted back. She moved the cursor to 'send'.

Melvyn Sparks's girlfriend Trudy didn't become anxious until thirty-six hours after the train took off. She had rung and got Melvyn's mobile's answerphone but that meant no more than that, as usual, his phone wasn't topped up. But when he didn't pitch up at her flat as arranged she began to worry.

Melvyn was occasionally unreliable, but not where football was concerned and tonight Chelsea were playing. They always watched together when Chelsea played. Trying his mobile again, she found the answerphone was off and a dead silence greeted her.

Melvyn had a brother, Steve, whose number Trudy had, as he had texted her when Melvyn had had a nasty fall from his bike and was in A & E.

'Steve?'

'Who's that?'

'Trudy. Melvyn's Trudy.'

'Hi, how you doing?'

'Have you heard from Melvyn – only he's not here and it's Chelsea playing.'

'Yeah, I know.'

'You haven't heard from him?'

'No, sorry.'

'Who's that, then?' Steve's girlfriend asked.

'Melvyn's girlfriend. Reckon he's dumped her and hasn't told her yet.'

'You do that with me and I'll cut your balls off.'

Melvyn had got to work early, because he was planning to help himself to a few sandwiches and he needed to get there before anyone else in order to fix the fridge. If the fridge was off he could waste enough of the cold food for supper that evening with Trudy. He was short because he'd been on the betting machines the night before, trying to make up for what he'd lost the night before that. In fact, he was badly in debt and had already borrowed from lolly.com. To be met by Monika, therefore, was a set-back.

'Hey, Melvyn!'

'Monika, oh hi.'

'You are an early bird.' Monika's preternaturally swift grasp of idiomatic English suggested an IQ well above that required for a buffet trolley. In fact, her vocabulary often stumped Melvyn. Today he noted she had a book sticking out of her shoulder bag.

'What you reading?'

'It is a very nice book called *Nineteen Eighty-Four*. I got it from the Oxfam shop. You know it?'

Melvyn, who was reading *Guardians of the Galaxy*, feigned interest. 'Good, yeah?'

'It is about Big Brother.'

'Oh, right.'

'Not the TV programme, of course. They, I think, have stolen the name from this book.'

'Yeah?'

'In my country it was banned.'

'Cool.'

'So it must be good. They only banned books that were good, you know?'

'Right. I got to, er, see to the . . .'

'Of course.'

Monika's clear grey eyes had a knowing expression,

but then they habitually had and, Melvyn told himself, perhaps he felt it more because he was feeling guilty. He was not a naturally dishonest man. Just one of many trying to make a living while life seemingly soared past him, sweeping up Russian criminals and property developers in its rich train.

He was making his way towards the buffet kitchen when the carriage jolted violently.

'Whoa. Driver must've got here.'

'I do not think so.' Monika was smiling now; her eyes, whose grey irises were encircled with a darker tinge, seemed alight with something like amusement.

November Night 7 was progressing but Nan hadn't yet decided what to do about the wolf. It lurked in the upper-right-hand corner, and it seemed to her that its expression took on varying aspects, sometimes menacing, sometimes wary, sometimes almost pleading even.

She was strangely unbothered by a manifestation so apparently independent of her artistic intent. Whatever it was it had arrived in her painting, and it seemed to belong there. So, she reflected, let it be.

Her laptop pinged and she walked over to it in some excitement, guessing the sender.

'I should be delighted to see more of your work,' the email ran. 'If you would kindly suggest some dates I shall hope we find one mutually convenient.'

He was certainly polite.

There was nothing at all in her diary. She never made engagements and even when she did generally she forgot to put them in her diary – or forgot to look if she had noted them there.

The phone rang and it was Matt.

'What are you doing?'

'Nothing. Why?' The question was so unlike Matt that she failed to notice that it was unlike her to fudge.

'I was thinking of coming home.'

'Oh.'

'You don't sound pleased.' Not for the first time Nan noticed how those who are regular in their habits become irrationally annoyed when a departure from them causes upset.

'Not not pleased. Just surprised. I've never known you take a day off work without planning weeks in advance.'

'I suppose I'm allowed to come back to my own home once in a while,' Matt said and rang off.

He appeared to have recovered his temper by the time she opened the door to him, looking abject.

'Darling, how lovely,' she said, kissing him with an enthusiasm assumed to hide annoyance at having had her day interrupted.

'Sorry to snap. I've got an awful head.'

That really wasn't like Matt. 'Poor love. Would you like tea and paracetamol?'

'Have we got any aspirin? I've got a fever. I think I might lie down.'

The presence of her husband uncharacteristically prone in bed in the house contributed to Nan's hesitation over the reply to Peter Randall. Quite why this was she could not have explained. Perhaps no more than the certainty that Matt would disapprove of the communication.

None the less, after further dithering, she sent an email offering Peter Randall some possible dates when he might choose to visit her studio.

The train had rattled along its usual route and then, so far as Melvyn could tell, it veered off on to a branch line. The line had once been the one that ran westwards across England, calling at the many small local stations that had got the chop in the bad old days of Dr Beeching. Naturally, Melvyn was too young to know, or care, who Beeching was. But Morris Foot, one of the train guards, an old union man, who claimed a family connection with Michael Foot, had rehearsed the evils of the Beeching cuts so regularly that Melvyn found he knew them.

Unless he had taken leave of his senses – and of course he might have done – that was Corsham they were passing. He knew Corsham because his mother's second husband had come from there. But the line that Corsham had been on had been closed for many years.

Monika, who had been busy in the kitchenette by the bar, now reappeared with a packet of Cheddars and two cans of Red Bull.

'I do not take fizzy drinks as a rule because of the sugar content but Red Bull is not so harmful. I read this in the *Daily Mail*.'

Melvyn was frankly grateful for any succour. His financial position had for some days necessitated a breakfast of dry cornflakes and even these were running to mere crushed crumbs. 'Oh, cheers.'

'Would you like to have sex with me?' Monika asked.

Matt's 'head' had become a raging fever, so Nan had called the GP.

'The surgery is closed from 6 a.m. to 8.30 a.m. Please dial this number after hours.'

She dialled the number, which advised her that there would be a wait of up to twenty minutes, and suggested that in any emergency she go to the nearest Accident & Emergency Department.

'Darling, they suggest going to an A & E.'

'Over my dead body. There are four-hour waits there. I could die in the corridor. Just give me some more aspirin.'

'I think you're over the limit, aren't you?'

'For Christ's sake. That's there to protect them from law suits. You can mainline the stuff before it does any real harm.'

With Matt asleep, snoring unhealthily and his face disconcertingly askew, Nan went back to her studio to inspect *November Night 7*. The wolf had definitely grown in substance. It now stood, balanced on high narrow legs, staring out of the canvas.

'What do you want?' Nan asked. 'What are you doing in my painting?'

'But we can't have simply lost an entire train?'

The Minister for Roads and Rail was close to tears. This was his first cabinet appointment. He had crept upwards in the party ranks by a combination of rapid coat-turning, lickspittle flattery and, finally the most effective, ditching his wife of twenty-four years for a young PA said to have the Prime Minister's ear. The ear had been cautiously receptive, but he was aware that in being given this undeniably testing post his mettle was being tried. The country's communications were in confusion. A spate of serious flooding had wrecked several main lines. The calculated cost of the proposed new high-speed train had rocketed, so that the treasury had privately shaken its collective head and urged that it be permanently 'postponed'. Unseasonal ice following the floods had made mincemeat of many major roads, including the older motorways. And, most mysterious of all, across the countryside massive molehills had appeared, breaking up the surfaces of minor roads and by-ways.

A tentative proposal to reopen some of the existing canals as a means of shifting heavy goods had been thwarted by the appearance of a strange strain of pond-weed which had engulfed all the waterways, making transport there problematic. And all the airports had in turn been closed due to high winds. Unquestionably, the communication system of Great Britain was foundering.

'It can't have vanished into thin air?' the Minister added.

'There's no trace of it, Minister. Just disappeared off the map.'

'For Christ's sake, that's impossible. It's Ted, by the way. Surely some bloody environmentalist group must have collared it.'

The civil servant, hardened by years of ministerial tantrums, was not inclined to be soothing. He rather enjoyed watching the new Minister flap.

'There's no sign of one, sir. And environmentalists are mostly keen on trains.'

'What about the buffet staff? Have they turned up?'

'Not as yet, Minister.'

'Do stop calling me that. Well, can't they be part of some, I don't know, terrorist gang?'

'The Home Office says they're looking into it.'

His ex-wife's best friend was the wife of the Home Secretary, who, he had heard on the grapevine, had counselled against his appointment.

'Let's hope they turn something up.'

'Nothing has been reported so far.'

'Trains don't vanish into thin air, man.' The Minister fell back on repetition.

'You'd think not, Minister. But it seems this one has.'

This is karma for dumping Moira, the Minister thought to himself.

Although Melvyn adopted a traditional bullish attitude to women when among his male peers, he was at heart, as is more often the way than not, scared of women. The reason he was with Trudy was simply that she had decided that he should be, and decisions, even unpalatable ones, come as a relief to the faint-hearted. The invitation to have sex with a curvaceous foreigner in a train that had apparently gone off the rails was profoundly disturbing to Melvyn. But it followed that he didn't want to seem rude.

'Erm, sure,' he said.

If his reply lacked enthusiasm, Monika didn't seem to register it. Or maybe it was simply that she didn't care. 'Good. The first-class carriages are best for this, I think.'

Lying across two passenger seats with Monika astride him, Melvyn could vaguely see countryside whizzing past through the opposite window. There appeared to be pine trees. Perhaps they were in one of the wooded regions of Wales.

Monika bent down and bit his ear so hard that he jerked in pain. 'You are coming?' she inquired.

'Oh, not yet. Sorry.'

'I will wait for you,' Monika said, leaning back on her heels.

By the time he was in a position to observe the passing scenery again, there seemed to be mountains. 'Where are we?' Melvyn adjusted his trousers.

Monika was mopping herself. 'You like one?' She offered a packet of baby wipes.

'Oh, thanks.'

'Sex with me was satisfactory?' Monika asked.

'Oh, yeah. Very nice, thank you.'

'I am good at sex,' Monika averred. 'My boyfriend would like me to be a porn star. But I am going to train at the Regency College to be an accountant. One of my gentlemen friends gave me money for the fees. When I have completed my training he would like me to work for his haulage business.'

Melvyn was staring out of the window. 'Isn't that snow?'

'Yes. I think maybe we are in Bavaria.'

'Bavaria?'

'I went to Bavaria with my boyfriend from Łódź. It was like this. Would you like maybe some more Red Bull?'

Nan felt obliged to keep an eye on Matt, who was looking most unwell, but she found it hard to keep away from the studio. She hurried back to her canvas after giving him lemon barley water. Nothing had changed but the wolf looked more alive than ever.

'What do you want?' she asked again.

The creature looked back at her. Slowly the yellow eyes blinked.

'Are you going to stay there?' Nan asked.

The wolf shook itself. Then it turned and padded into the painted darkness.

The phone rang.

'Hello?'

'Mrs Maitland?'

'Yes.'

'Peter Randall.'

'Oh, hello.'

'Would this evening be convenient at all?'

Walking back to the house again, Nan thought, But I didn't give him my number. Maybe Austin gave it to him. Perhaps I shouldn't have said he could come, with Matt so ill. She turned back to the studio and dialled 1471 to get Peter Randall's number. 'You were called today at 3.47,' the voice intoned. 'The caller withheld their number.'

Oh, well, Nan thought. What will be will be.

'The Home Office rang finally, Minister.'

'Why the hell didn't you put them through to me?'

'Nothing to report, Minister. They've drawn a

48

complete blank on the buffet staff. He's a harmless chap, no record of anything except some shoplifting as a juvenile, and she's a Polish immigrant with nothing dodgy to her name.'

'And what about the train?'

'Not a dicky bird, Minister.'

'God knows what's going on.'

'Let's hope someone does, Minister.'

'But how did we get here?' Melvyn asked, with little expectation of an answer. Distracted as he'd been by Monika's sexual athleticism, he was certain they had not gone under any sea.

Monika had seemingly lost all interest in him once the sex was over. If Melvyn had been able to make his inchoate thoughts conscious, he might have complained that he had always supposed that it was men who became indifferent to their partners after sex. But maybe this wasn't so for Poles. However, these unexpressed reactions were wholly submerged beneath a mounting panic. 'What's going on?' he pleaded.

Monika peered out of the window. 'We'll be there soon.'

'But where? Where's there?' Melvyn was almost crying now.

'Where we are going,' Monika said calmly. 'And there we will make babies.'

'But you have a boyfriend, you said.'

'He does not want any babies.'

'I don't want any babies either.'

'This is not important. When I have the babies you can go.'

The ambulance had left and Nan was gathering together Matt's things to follow after it to the hospital. The sight of his violently flushed face and stertorous breathing when she had gone up to bed had frankly alarmed her. She had put wet flannels on his face and chest but from the feel of his skin his temperature had risen so high that finally, braving his probably future protests, she had rung the emergency services. It was an hour and forty minutes, and felt like a fortnight, before they arrived.

'Apologies, Mrs er, we got sent to the wrong post code. They get these Eastern Europeans on the desk. Can't tell their w's from their v's.'

'Suppose my husband had died while we were waiting for you?'

'I can't say it doesn't happen but it wouldn't be us to blame. It'd be the migrants they hire that can't speak the Queen's English.'

Oh, great, Nan thought. Matt could be dead of racial prejudice. Dolefully, she packed pyjamas, underpants, socks and Matt's washing things, wondering as she did so when he had begun to wear pyjamas. For some years now, she supposed. In the beginning they had always slept naked. Please don't die, Matt, she thought. I'm sorry if I've ever found you annoying.

But any potential tragedy has an element of excitement about it. Driving back from the hospital, where Matt had been set up with an antibiotic drip, she found herself unwilling to return home and veered off towards the park. Too bad if Peter Randall turned up at the house.

She had been in the park at night many times and had relished the lively hush and the pleasing smell of damp vegetation. Parking the car by Cumberland Lodge (where she had attended an art history course when they first moved to Windsor), she stepped into the November night.

Somewhere a creature yowled and there were sounds of nocturnal birds and scurrying movements in the trees above. The moon was out, and stars punctured the high skies with a clarity which seemed to Nan to signal an existence free from mortal care. A kind of exultation began to fizzle through her body. Wrung through with anxiety as she was, she none the less felt unusually alive.

So when a piece of the low-lying bush detached itself and began to pace towards her, she was not afraid. Her bones had told her what it was. The wolf, her wolf. Nan stood there, in its path, making no sound.

The wolf stopped in front of her, leaving a space of about a metre between them. Then it turned and walked back down the path.

Nan followed at a slight distance. The moon, lacking

the stars' exquisite brilliance, was shrouded in a gauze of luminous mist, and across its veiled face a tracery of cloud was scudding making the trees' long shadows flicker and dance wantonly beside her. Suddenly she remembered her godmother telling her that that phenomenon was known as 'a wind on the moon' and whatever you did that night you were doomed to repeat for a whole year. She was not afraid but a strangeness clung about her heart, as if some fate that had lain always in wait for her was about to be revealed.

Overnight, Matt Maitland found himself in an underground cave. Stalactites hung from the cave's roof and beneath his feet crunched shale of many-coloured minerals. His old professor, Malcolm Hertford, from University College, greeted him and advised him that he was being awarded the Nobel Prize.

'But for what?'

'They wanted to give it to you jointly with me, but I persuaded them that the younger man should have it. Youth before wisdom. Youth before wisdom. Besides, I'm dead, you know.'

'Did I come to your funeral?' Matt felt some anxiety. He had a bad feeling that he'd neglected to go.

'You came with Lily,' his professor said, smiling.

'You mean, Nan?'

'Not at all. Your assistant, Lily.'

Did I have an assistant named Lily? Matt wondered.

Perhaps she was the redhead he'd rather fancied. But surely she was called Veronica. Nan had been jealous of her and he had lied in describing her as ugly and then felt guilty for the lie.

Pondering this, he noticed that he seemed to have acquired evening dress and patent leather shoes. Never in his life had he worn patent leather.

He stirred restlessly as a nurse adjusted the drip in his arm.

'I don't deserve it,' he murmured.

'It will pass,' the nurse reassured him. She was one of the older generations of nurses, trained to offer solicitude as well as drugs. 'It'll all seem better by morning.'

'But I've done nothing. Nothing,' Matt protested.

'I know, my love. Life isn't fair,' the nurse soothed. Her own daughter had died as an infant from meningitis and her husband had for years been disabled with Parkinson's. She was an old hand at fielding life's knocks.

Meantime, Professor Hertford was pinning medals on to Matt's unwilling chest. A pin stuck into him and he moaned louder.

'Be a man about it,' the Professor advised. 'Put your shoulders back. Look sharp.'

'But it hurts,' Matt moaned.

'There, there,' the nurse consoled. She stroked her patient's forehead, sticky with sweat. It was nearing dawn and soon she would leave the poor man with the day staff. Years of dealing with the disadvantages of a

Caribbean lineage had not immured her against her own brand of prejudice. She was frankly mistrustful of the new breed of foreign nurse.

At Cumberland Lodge there was consternation over what appeared to be a night raid on the kitchens. The fridge had been emptied of the venison steaks that were thawing there, ready for a dinner that evening at which the Minister for Science and Education was due to speak on government policy on genetic engineering. Moreover, the remains of the carcass and the tines of a young stag's antlers were found by an abandoned car near the lodge gates. The car's owner, a Mrs Nancy Maitland, was nowhere to be found, and police inquiry revealed that her next of kin was dangerously ill in Wexham Park Hospital.

And rumours began to spread that two of the royal park keepers had sighted animals resembling wolves. 'Not so much "resembling" I should say,' a senior keeper asserted to a younger colleague. 'Those were wolves they were, or I'm Lady Gaga.'

'Going gaga, more like,' joked his colleague, who in truth was feeling alarm and sought to abate it by having a bit of a go at old John.

Dr Matt Maitland was being awarded the Nobel Prize for Literature.

'But I don't write,' he was protesting.

'This is the only way we can award you the prize.' The

official nodded towards Professor Hertford, who beamed and nodded back, silently clapping his hands.

'It will save the world,' his professor explained. 'Reason must go underground. The philistines are upon us. All for one and one for all.'

'God help us!' Matt groaned.

'We should call his wife,' the night nurse was saying. 'He's been crying out like that all night.'

'Raving?' asked the day nurse.

The night nurse pursed her lips. 'It's not a word I'd like to use, poor soul.'

Before leaving the room she kissed her crucifix. She was a natural intuitive and recognized when a patient was not long for this world.

Nan was taken by Peter Randall (if that is who it was) to meet those who had decided that Britain must be, roots upwards, reformed. She never actually saw them, for, he intimated, these were powers which disdained the vulgarity of assuming mortal shape. But she understood that the British Isles were about to undergo a radical restructuring: an ecological experiment, a test case, in short, for further global developments. A major reformation through reforestation was already in progress, and wild life, in all its time-honoured, ancient forms, would be taking over the cities and towns.

Quite why she had been chosen to escape the consequences of centuries of human mismanagement she never discovered. Judging by the poor young man in tow with the voluptuous Polish beauty, and the elderly Jamaican nurse, who were also present at the meeting, it seemed likely it was mere random chance. But perhaps this was part of the new order – a different way of evaluating people. The human race, she understood, was anyway being demoted. And why shouldn't the governance of the world be run on random lines after all?

She did ask about her husband and was told only that he had been chosen to introduce a fatal virus into the community. From the manner in which this news was conveyed to her, she gathered it was considered to be something of an honour.

Mown Grass

———◄o►———

All flesh is grass . . .
— Isaiah 40:6

'But,' said Eileen Stanbridge, 'there remains the question of Robinson.'

She was with her two daughters, in the well-shelved library of the family country home that, after long wranglings, she had decided (though God knew it would probably kill her) had to be sold. They had agonized over the sale, she and her daughters, Tessa and Ginny, but, in the end, it really seemed the only option.

Robin Stanbridge, Eileen's husband, had died days after his retirement from the family firm for which he had worked dutifully for over fifty years. Privately, he had detested the work. As a young man, he had excelled at golf and had nursed an ambition to become a professional. He had also possessed a fine baritone voice, for which, at university, he had been applauded in productions of Gilbert and Sullivan, and had dreamt, at times, about the possibility of going on, after he graduated, to music school.

But the weight of family tradition, a certain faintheartedness in his character and an inherited belief that he needed money to be happy had strapped him to the wheel of Stanbridge & Turnbull, an engineering firm that in recent years had specialized, very profitably, in road construction in the Third World.

Road construction, however uninspiring, had provided Robin Stanbridge with an income large enough to buy a substantial country house in Kent, along with a roomy London flat in a smart Bloomsbury square.

His daughters had been educated at one of the better, certainly more expensive boarding schools, and they had returned this investment by marrying young businessmen who could, as it seemed, keep them in the style of life they had grown to expect.

Events had routed that expectation. One of the sons-in-law, Jeremy, started a wine company that went bust and took irrevocably to drink himself (which, Eileen Stanbridge liked to intimate, had perhaps precipitated the crisis in the first place). At his father-in-law's expense, he attended several rehab programmes, each time with a renewed but deceptive enthusiasm for personal reform. Finally, he retreated into perpetual alcoholic unemployment, leaving Robin to provide for his two children.

Robin's other son-in-law, Tessa's husband, Terence, belatedly came out, gave up his City job with an international finance firm and went off with his new partner to run an organic restaurant in Shropshire. Terence was punctilious about paying for the children but when times turned hard and the restaurant profits faltered, yet again Robin found himself the only stable financial resource for a daughter.

Robin loved his daughters, and their children, but he sometimes wondered how they had managed to select for their partners in life such unreliable providers. He came to resent, without ever giving voice to the fact, the burden imposed on him by the assumption that his only role in life was to be the family 'money bags'.

This feeling unexpressed over the years gathered force. He began to give rein to his secret desire for insurrection by playing riskily on the stock exchange. When he died, after a strenuous game of golf, in which he was supposedly celebrating his new-found freedom from road construction, it was days after learning that there would be very little beyond his pension to provide for retirement. It was perhaps as well that the heart attack occurred before he could face explaining the situation to his wife.

Eileen Manning had been a tall, fair, handsome girl when Robin had married her. She had been a reliable doubles partner at tennis, with a strong serve which saw them winning their club mixed doubles, and had an extroverted manner at parties which he had mistaken for a larger good will. She seemed promisingly keen on sex until after the honeymoon. They had been home from Lemnos two weeks when she announced that she preferred to sleep alone, with her dogs.

Robin Stanbridge dealt with this blow as he dealt with most things, quietly. Having done what he suspected was his duty, in fathering Tessa and Virginia, he began to look for a woman, kind enough, and willing enough, to provide him with a measure of sexual happiness and relieve his wife of the nuisance of shooing the dogs from her bed in order to accommodate her husband. In all other respects, he was a loyal spouse – except for the matter of the gambling on the stock market.

The discovery of her husband's perfidy in this department, the very one she had always counted on as most reliable, surmounted any shock Eileen had felt at his death. She called her daughters for a family council at their country home. All three women, who were otherwise inclined to quarrel, were united in damning Robin's negligence. They had taken for granted a lifelong ride on the gravy train and felt that their resentment at its derailment was wholly justified.

After many expressions of anger and self-directed grief, they reached, or Eileen did, the painful decision. The house in Kent must be sold. Eileen would permanently relocate to the London flat. Ginny, the younger daughter, who had been perched in one of the flat's rooms for nine years, would have to find other accommodation. The decision prompted renewed expressions of outrage. One source of outrage was a provision in Robin's will. He had left, they were informed by his solicitor, a legacy to the woman who had seen to the

Kent house for thirty-one years. A woman known generally as Mrs Robinson.

'I can't understand it. Robin hardly spoke to her. I don't believe he even knew her first name.'

'I don't know it either,' Ginny said.

'It's Margaret.' Of the three, Tessa was the most democratic. Until recently, she had prided herself on a small rebellion against the family's known political sympathies by voting Lib Dem. 'But she calls herself Peggy.'

The mother of Eileen Stanbridge, who had risen in life to marry Henry Manning, Bart., had never forgiven her own mother for having been a lady's maid. To establish her distance from that position, she had addressed all her staff by their surname. 'Robinson' was the way her mother would have addressed their 'help', and when speaking of her, if not to her face directly, Eileen unconsciously followed her mother's example. But to everyone else in the household, from the day she arrived, she was 'Mrs Robinson'.

The day she arrived, in answer to an advert in the local Post Office shop, was, as it happened, a day when Eileen Stanbridge was not at home. If Eileen no longer recalled this fact, it was because the arrival of Peggy Robinson was, as with everything about her, unassuming.

It was Robin Stanbridge who had received and interviewed her in his study one weekend when his wife had gone off to a dog show. And perhaps because he was alone, and relieved of the usual constraining effects of his wife's presence, he found himself joking gently with the prospective 'help' about the slight congruence of their names.

'I can't really turn you down with a name like yours,' he had said, with the humorous turn to his mouth which had once caused his wife to form the view that he was not unattractive. 'Seeing my own name is Robin.'

Peggy Robinson also had an attractive smile, though few were privileged to see it.

'What's your name?' Robin continued. He had enjoyed the smile. 'Your first name, I mean?'

'Margaret. But I'm known mostly as Peggy.'

'Well, Peggy, I think you'll suit us. D'you think we'll suit you?'

Eileen Stanbridge had insisted, naturally, on seeing for herself the young woman whom Robin had believed they might employ. She did not ask her first name. But she read her references, which were positive, from the local family who were moving to France and regretted they therefore had to let her go. Nor could Eileen afford to be too fussy. Their previous 'help' had left after a row about cleaning up after the spaniels, and the house in her absence was becoming unmanageable.

As her husband had learnt, for Eileen Stanbridge finding fault was a source of daily energy, as regular and fortifying as her breakfast egg; but, even for her, it was hard to find any fault with Mrs Robinson. She arrived punctually, three mornings a week, in the early days in a pale blue Hillman (always meticulously clean), later in a small Toyota, stayed on, if requested, for dinner parties, and the clearing up afterwards, and was not apparently inconvenienced when Eileen's elderly spaniel, Queenie, had diarrhoea while sleeping in her mistress's bed.

Their 'help' presented her person uncontroversially too: always wearing some version of a flowered wraparound overall, her rather small feet clad unexceptionally, according to the weather and the seasons, either in moccasin slippers or sandals.

Her fine, wavy, hair was a dark shade of mouse, and even with increasing age showed no interpolating grey. She wore no distinguishable makeup other than an occasional slick of lipstick. Her only truly distinctive marks were her eyes, which were a peculiarly vivid blue, and the scent which at some unidentifiable point she began to wear. When Tessa once complimented her on it, Mrs Robinson replied that her nephew bought it for her from a shop in London, adding that she couldn't remember the shop's name.

It is not possible to be entirely ignorant of someone who comes into your household for many years on a thrice-weekly basis. It became known that Mrs Robinson lived in a modern yellow-brick house on a purpose-built estate in a nondescript village of no historical significance, ten miles from theirs. It was taken for granted she would spend her annual holidays with her sister in the Lake District and she had mentioned a friend in London whom she visited at weekends. If she had any strong attachment to another human soul it appeared to be to her sister's son, who was apparently the source of the few items of luxury she occasionally displayed: a rather fine enamelled brooch, worked as a speedwell; a silver bracelet; and the unusual scent.

That was the sum of notice that Peggy Robinson had attracted in the family until the content of Robin Stanbridge's will was made known.

'What is it exactly he's left her, anyway?' Ginny asked. Of the two girls she was the more put out by her father's financial treachery. She owned a small flat in Brixton, but for the last nine years had let it and had come to think of the flat in Bloomsbury Square as her own.

'It seems to be a London freehold with a couple of leaseholds. Not terribly valuable, only bringing in a hundred or so a year, but still.'

'What was Daddy doing with that?'

'Presumably he thought it was an investment.' She should, Eileen thought angrily, have been keeping an eye on all this.

'A bloody nerve, isn't it, not leaving it to you, Mummy, or us? Especially with all he hasn't left us.'

Eileen Stanbridge thought so too and had inquired from the solicitor as to the exact nature of the title. It appeared to have been purchased twenty years earlier and held the leases of two properties, a shop and a two-bedroom flat overhead. Both leases had over a hundred years to run.

'Why has he left it to her? Daddy hadn't gone bonkers, had he?'

Eileen had also made inquiries on that score. There had been other wills, which she had known of and indeed believed she had been party to. This one was of fairly recent date: a mere two years before the fatal episode.

'Was she in the earlier wills?' Eileen had asked. David Saxby, their long-standing solicitor, affirmed that this particular legacy was, he believed, of some duration. Other beneficiaries of past wills, Cousin Olive and her two sons, for example, had, from his recollection, been removed from the list of beneficiaries but not, in the final analysis, it would seem, Mrs Robinson.

Eileen didn't waste any time feeling grateful for the jettisoning of Cousin Olive.

'I don't believe she was "Mrs" or has a husband at all!' She was aware that her solicitor was wordlessly advising her that any challenge to the will would be legally unsustainable.

So now there was the question of what to do with 'Mrs' Robinson with the will read and her new, and incomprehensible, position known. Should they keep her on to help dismantle the house? It was hardly possible to envisage managing the task without her. And yet, to ask a legatee, one who had been promised a regular if slender income when their own position was so perilous, seemed to them mortifying.

In the end, the question was left unaddressed. Peggy Robinson came as usual three times a week to help prepare for the move. Nothing was said on either side about the legacy. Nor did either Eileen or Ginny ask about her future plans.

Tessa alone touched on the subject, asking if Mrs Robinson was likely to move away, as she, Tessa, knew of some people looking for a reliable 'help'. Among the family, she had loved the dead man best and had tried to suggest that if the stock market had failed he could not be held solely to blame. Her loyalty had been slapped down by her mother and her sister. But she also held a vague fondness for Mrs Robinson.

Peggy Robinson's answer was also vague. 'I'm considering my options.'

'So, have you been to see the shop and the flat?' Tessa risked.

Peggy Robinson was kneeling on the floor by the elm chest that had belonged to Cousin Olive, from which she was sorting out linen. She looked up at Tessa, who had forgotten how her eyes were so very blue. Without a word, their 'help' looked down into the chest and continued sorting.

The first time that Robin Stanbridge kissed Peggy Robinson was almost by accident.

He had damaged a toe playing golf with an ill-fitting shoe. The toe had flared up, and hobbling into the kitchen one Saturday he had encountered Peggy, who had come in to clear after a dinner party the evening before.

Robin had taken a modest pride in having been the one who had led to their employing their 'help' in the first place. If he had consciously forgotten her smile on that occasion, the effect of it had made a small imprint on his memory. He explained to her the reason for the hobbling and she suggested he soak the toe in a bowl of boiled water and boric acid. 'You don't want it going septic. I've done a first-aid course,' she explained. 'I passed with distinction.' This, which in another woman might have been taken for a mild boast, was purely to reassure him.

Robin responded positively to any reassurance, which for most of his life had been in short supply. He sat down, took off his sock and rolled up his trousers. As their 'help' rose from setting the bowl of water down by his feet, their heads somehow collided, so that he found himself seizing her face in his two hands to see that she wasn't hurt.

The gesture ended in a kiss which embarrassed them both. Nothing at all was said at the time, but Robin Stanbridge found himself wanting to repeat the accident.

Some weeks later, Eileen took the girls up to town to

see *The Sound of Music* for Ginny's eleventh birthday. At Eileen's request, Mrs Robinson had come in, in her employer's absence, to give the dog hair in her bedroom 'a good going over'. Robin, having been advised of this scheme by his wife, quite deliberately entered her bedroom, and, finding their 'help' stooped to vacuum under the bed, clasped her firmly round the hips.

She did not resist the embrace. Her hipbones, in Robin's grip, felt to him pleasingly bony. They retired to his bedroom and both were surprised by the passion they shared.

Peggy at that time was thirty-two. She was not in fact married, nor had she ever been. She had been engaged for a time to a soldier who got a casual encounter pregnant and was dragooned by her family into marrying the girl.

Her soldier's dereliction hurt Peggy and had left her cautious over love affairs. But the real loss was the soldier's, because, of the two women, Peggy was the more ardent.

It was an ardour which, with no other outlet, had gathered momentum over time and it sparked Robin Standbridge's own unignited passion. The two found themselves in the lucky position of making a natural erotic fit. Further sessions of love-making swiftly followed the first. Once, one late June evening – it became a kind of legendary joke between them – in the middle of the rolling lawn, newly cut by Robin, they had made passionate love, an occasion given spice by the fact that Eileen was expected back any minute from London. Lying back with her face in his neck, shreds of grass in his still-thick hair, Robin had said, 'Peg, this can't go on. I want to make love to you in the grass any time I like.'

But, with the inevitable fading of the splendour in the grass, Robin lacked the moral courage to desert his wife. And Peggy was too unassuming to demand that he try.

However, they continued to delight each other. Sometimes he gave her little gifts, which she took a sly pleasure in flaunting as she cleaned at the Stanbridges': the figured enamelled brooch, a speedwell, 'blue like your eyes', he told her; the silver bracelet; and, more daringly, as bolstered by her desire for him Robin acquired confidence, silk underwear. The last she sometimes wore beneath her demure work overalls, coming into his study to give him a tantalizing glimpse.

There came a point when Robin felt he wanted more control over his affair than his wife's capricious time-table allowed. Passing an estate agent's office in Marylebone High Street, after a routine check-up with his cardiologist, he saw in their window EXCELLENT INVESTMENT OPPORTUNITY. FREEHOLD OF MARYLEBONE HIGH STREET SHOP WITH LEASEHOLD FLAT ABOVE.

He investigated the shop, which proved to sell scents based on natural products. On a rare impulse, he bought for Peggy one of their products, a scent called 'New Mown Grass', a memory of their daring lawn encounter.

The scent, in his imagination, bestowed on the shop an erotic aura. Inquiry revealed that it was leased for a hundred and twenty-five years but that the lease of the flat above had only forty to run. The price of the freehold at the time was comparatively cheap, and Robin's role as family financier gave him unimpeded control.

He bought the freehold and rented the flat from the leaseholder, who was frankly glad to have it off his hands. The flat became a meeting place with Peggy, where they spent weekends, when Robin was supposedly on business trips, making love, or, increasingly with the years, watching DVDs and companionably doing the crossword.

Peggy by this time had revealed some surprising talents. She was, it appeared, a first-rate bridge player; she also, with her nephew, played chess. Because she was interested, and no one in his family was, Robin introduced her to the stock market and the games one could play with stocks and shares.

After one successful stock market gamble, one he had discussed in depth with Peggy, he bought out the leaseholder and put the flat in her name.

By the time Robin came to retire, he had reached a decision. He would leave Eileen after all. She could have the country house and the Bloomsbury flat, and he would retire with Peggy to the modest little flat in Marylebone High Street. It would entail a row – the biggest and most taxing of his life. But he was willing to undergo this for the promise of comfort in his last years. The prospect of living them out in the crampingly critical atmosphere of his marriage, unrelieved by absence at work, and the cover that work had given him, was sufficiently grim to bring on this late resolution. And, while Eileen would assuredly give him hell, there was enough money to make the parting ultimately not too disagreeable.

Soon after Robin made this decision the world markets crashed and with them Robin's prospect of a life of independence.

David Saxby had been tactful over the details of the legacy to Peggy Robinson. An examination of the leasehold particulars would have revealed her name, Margaret Audrey Robinson, on the Marylebone High Street flat. But Eileen Stanbridge, having recognized that there was nothing to be gained by questioning her late husband's soundness of mind, had let the matter drop, with no less inner disgust but without further investigation.

Tessa, however, remained curious. With her father's death, she found she wanted to know him better. One afternoon, months after probate had been granted, she took the Central line to Bond Street and walked up the Marylebone High Street.

Halfway up, she found the shop, 'Completely Natural', which advertised in its window display NATURAL SCENTS FOR A MORE NATURAL YOU.

The space inside the shop was small but smelt delicious. A number of tester sprays were available on the enticingly arranged shelves. Tessa examined the labels: 'Honeysuckle', 'Violet', 'Meadow Sweet', 'New Mown Grass'.

Once probate had been granted, Peggy put her house on the market and moved into the flat over 'Completely Natural'. In the light of the stock market crash she had decided to put the proceeds of the house sale into preference shares, which, as she had learnt, provided an unfluctuating income.

At the first opportunity, she presented herself at the shop, explaining to the owner, who knew her from the visits with Robin, that she was planning to live overhead permanently. She was, she said, looking for some local employment, and if by chance there was anything she could do to help below it would be most convenient.

The owner, who was seeking to expand, was thrilled and soon Peggy was taken on as manager.

She enjoyed running downstairs each morning into the sweetly scented atmosphere, the welcome air of opulence in her new environment and the customers who matched its style. Above all, she liked the feeling of being in charge.

She missed Robin, but she would not have had things differently. Sometimes she saw his face, scarlet, puffy, his eyes mutely appealing as he collapsed on the kitchen floor that day he came home from playing golf as she was leaving his house for good.

'I can't go through with it, Peg,' he had said to her, the night before. 'You understand? We'll stay in touch. I'm sorry, but I can't afford it now.'

And she did understand. She understood that bullying and criticism and greed would always trump kindness and tenderness and loyalty, in the end. Perhaps she might have saved him had she applied the mouth-to-mouth resuscitation, had she thumped his heart as she had practised, all those years ago, at the first-aid class. Impossible to say. But even to try to save him for Eileen, for those monsters . . . she couldn't afford it now.

The Boy Who Could See Death

Eli was not quite seven years old when he discovered that he was different. But perhaps 'different' was not at the time, at least, the right word. For at that time, in most ways, he was a quite ordinary child, with the common traits, good and bad, and many in between, that ordinary little boys will have.

But in one important respect he differed from the ordinary.

Eli discovered this when, one March day, he looked into the eyes of his friend Thomas Wilkes and said, 'You are going to die on Tuesday.'

This pronouncement, delivered with unusual solemnity, naturally upset Tommy Wilkes, who was found by his mother in the garden crying and saying goodbye to his treehouse. She had words with Eli's mother, Mrs Faring, who took the complaint calmly. 'I'm sorry if Tommy was upset but boys will be boys. I'm sure it was just Eli's silly joke.'

But when Eli's mother spoke to her son about the matter, he looked at her in bewilderment. 'But he *is* going to die,' he said. 'He'll hit his head.'

'I've told you not to be fanciful,' said his mother

sharply, but in truth she was a little disconcerted. She spoke to Eli's father when he came home from work.

'Boys fooling around,' was his father's verdict. He was tired and wanted his regular evening beer and to be left in peace to watch the news. But when, the following Tuesday, after school, Tommy Wilkes fell from his tree-house and broke his neck, it was inevitable that questions were asked.

And it was just as inevitable that the distraught family of the dead boy should feel obliquely that Eli was some-how to blame. Although he had been nowhere near either Thomas or the treehouse when the accident occurred, it was suspected by the grieving family that the strange prediction must somehow have precipitated the tragedy.

Eli's parents questioned him themselves about the incident, but all Eli would say was, 'I saw it in his eyes.' Pressing him to expand on this proved useless. Eli had nothing to add.

The Wilkes family, unable to come to terms with their loss, sought solace in spreading malicious gossip about Eli's prophetic words. The atmosphere of recrimination became so marked that Eli was ostracized at school and his work began to suffer. Finally, he was discreetly moved to another school.

The singular event remained just that until one day, watching the news on TV, Eli looked into the eyes of the newly elected President of the United States and pronounced, 'That man is going to die.' His father, who had dismissed the episode with Thomas as an unlucky coincidence, chose to ignore this. Mothers, however, are generally more in touch with their children and it was not mere curiosity but some more pressing sense that prompted Mrs Faring to ask, 'When and how?'

'He will be shot,' Eli said, 'on . . .' and he named the exact day on which a shocked world learnt that President Kennedy had been assassinated.

The news, when it came, was doubly shocking to the Farings, who were forced to conclude that, in the words of Mrs Faring's mother, something was 'going on'. In view of the previous trouble, they felt that their son's bizarre prediction was best kept within the family. But they reckoned without Mrs Faring's mother.

'The boy has second sight.' Mrs Faring's mother made this pronouncement with a confidence born out of uncertainty in other areas of her life. She had only recently moved in with her daughter's family and was unsure of her position in this new, and not always friendly, environment. Unlike her daughter, she was ready to be proud of her grandson's gift, if he had one, and the news that he had foretold the death of the President of the United States was too good to overlook as a means of forging local alliances. Also, she wanted to get a bit of her own back on her son-in-law, who, she correctly guessed, had tried to veto her moving into the family home in the first place.

The news leaked out from Mrs Faring's mother's new cronies and spread through the neighbourhood like wild fire. One of the cronies had a son-in-law who was a journalist with a national paper. In a short time, the story had sparked a larger interest. The Faring parents, overwhelmed by the growing invasion of the press, and seriously rattled, moved away from the area after putting Mrs Faring's mother into a care home.

By now, Eli himself had become more cautious, so that when he one day looked at the face of Mr Lynch, the metalwork teacher at his new school, and saw in it an image of its owner's coming end, he said nothing but merely presented, on the morning of the day that was to be his teacher's last, a bunch of gloriously scented sweet peas from the Farings' garden.

The odd gesture – for flowers were not the usual currency of twelve-year-old schoolboys – did not go unremarked. That evening, the very one on which he was to die of a brain aneurism, Clive Lynch passed the flowers to his wife with the comment, 'Don't know what got into the kid who gave me these but he looked as if he was seeing a ghost.'

Maureen Lynch had been curious. 'What's the kid's name, then?'

At the funeral, Maureen Lynch spotted Eli with his parents and asked him if he might like to drop by sometime. Eli had been fond of his teacher and was experiencing the guilt which superior knowledge will often bring. So one afternoon, he showed up at their house, now woefully empty of Mr Lynch. 'Did you perhaps guess my husband was going to die?' his wife asked, when she had taken Eli into the kitchen and offered him milk and a chocolate digestive. 'Only, he told me it was you'd given him those flowers.'

Eli was a truthful boy. 'Yes,' he admitted and, sad and embarrassed, covered his face.

His teacher's widow, however, was intrigued rather than angry. 'How did you know?' and, when there was no answer, she persisted, 'What did you see? Was it in his eyes?'

When Eli was sixteen he fell head over heels in love with Iris Jackson. He had grown into a good-looking boy, with a head of jet-black hair and eyes 'blue as the high heavens', as his banished grandmother used to say, in the days she was still permitted to express a view on her only grandchild. Eli courted his love with the caution which had by now become second nature, never pushing too hard for what he wanted, so that by the time Iris was seventeen she was ready to go to the 'next stage', as in those days it was called.

But one fateful evening, catching sight of Iris's sister Debbie's month-old baby, Eli audibly drew in his breath. Asked why by the vigilant Iris, he at first refused to speak. But he was in love and his second thought was that the girl he hoped to marry was owed a perfect candour. So, heart in mouth, he explained what he feared he had seen reflected in the tiny infant's darkly shining pupils.

Iris's mother had disturbed Iris by suggesting that Eli often acted as though 'he had something to hide' and this sinister pronouncement from him further unnerved her. She became slower to answer his phone calls and soon an alternative interest, Wayne Healey, a well-muscled young man with a rugger background and no trace of 'something funny' about him, appeared. When Eli heard the tragic news that Debbie's baby girl had died of meningitis, he guessed that he would not hear from Iris again.

Time passed, and Eli learnt to conceal better what he saw when the mark of a coming death caught his unwilling eye. And with this concealment, as is the way, came other suppressions of spontaneity.

Eli's father, feeling ill at ease with a son apparently not evolving along traditional lines, became sarcastic and critical. That this stemmed from awkwardness rather than any real antipathy was no comfort to the boy, who, having withdrawn still more from contact with his peers, began to seem to his parents reserved and aloof and then even to become so with them.

When Eli read the telltale signs in his mother's face, he shaded his eyes from his father's behind the dark glasses he had taken to wearing and suggested to his mother a drive, the two of them, in his father's maroon Triumph Herald, to Box Hill. They walked there, recalling together,

fondly, their picnics as a family when he was a small boy
before . . . well, before everything of which neither of
them could speak. Then Eli removed himself to the
Welsh Marches, where he remained incommunicado for
a month, leaving his father to manage his wife's mortal
heart attack alone.

By this time, Eli was twenty-two and pretty much
friendless. The remoteness of the Welsh countryside
suited what had grown to be his temperament. He made
a living of sorts – a 'shiftless' one, his father called it, on
one of his son's few returns to the family home – with
casual labouring jobs and bits of skilled metalwork. For
the dead Mr Lynch had left his mark.

And if there is a universal sympathy in things, maybe
it was not so surprising that one day Eli encountered
Mrs Lynch, who had never forgotten the boy who had
predicted her husband's death. It was in fact metalwork
that brought them back in touch.

Eli had found a job helping out at the local garage,
where odd jobs of household repairs were also taken in.
This was in the days when not everyone automatically
replaced a leaky kettle or a saucepan that had lost its
handle, when kitchen items were made of reparable
substances, often, in Wales, anyhow, of iron or tin.

Maureen Lynch had the means to buy new. But she
had retained, as a kind of honouring of her dead first
husband, a belief in the virtue of 'making good'. A
saucepan, one she was fond of, had developed a shaky

handle and she had taken it round to Glen Brennan's garage to see if it could be set to rights.

When the gawky young man with jet-black hair and a protruding Adam's apple appeared from out the back to collect this article, she almost screamed with surprise, adding, more soberly, 'Eli, Eli Faring, isn't it?'

Eli had reverted to his full name Eliot, since he had found that the shortening by which he had been known from birth tended to give rise to anti-Semitic prejudices, and he felt he already had enough on his plate without adding that woe besides. He blushed. But he recognized the handsome, red-haired woman with the slightly protuberant blue eyes; and he recognized that she had recognized him as the boy who had given her dead husband the flowers.

'Mrs Lynch?' It may have been flattering that she remembered him but his anonymity had become a protective fleece and he was disturbed by this interloper from his past.

'Merrill now. Lynch as was. What are you doing in this backwater, Eli?' It was as if she knew he had changed his name and was determined not to let him forget who he really was.

'This and that.'

Maureen Merrill's second marriage had strengthened up her bossy side. 'You'd better come round to our place for a bite of supper and say what you've been up to, Eli Faring.'

Eli went. 'Any port in a storm,' he said to himself,

quoting one of the favourite maxims of the grand-mother who had unwittingly set him on the desolate path of alienation.

Frank Merrill was proud of his brisk, good-looking wife who had brought order into a previously ragbag existence. He was intrigued rather than alarmed by her story of the young boy – who had so remarkably fore-seen the death of her first husband when no one else had any idea that his health hung by a fraying thread – and was not at all averse to having Eli over to take a look at him. A kind of freak, his wife had intimated. And he had laughed. 'A weirdo, eh? Well, it takes all sorts.'

The Merrills lived in a roomy Welsh farmhouse from which Maureen Merrill ran a B and B, more for occupa-tion than for any financial need. The death of her first husband had left her with a substantial life insurance payout and Frank, who, with no dependants, had retired from his business marketing toys for Christmas crack-ers, commanded a reasonable pension.

Soon Eli was a frequent guest at the Merrills', and it didn't take long for Maureen to suggest one night, in bed after they'd had what Frank referred to as 'a bit of a cuddle', 'How about we have the boy take the spare room, Frankie? We don't have many guests and any that come can always go into the B and B wing.'

Eli moved into the Merrills' place with a tinge of reluctance. He had grown accustomed, if not recon-ciled, to isolation and feared too close a proximity to others. But there was no doubt that, after his Spartan accommodation over the garage, the room at the Merrills', with its own washbasin and a fine view over Offa's Dyke, was a lure.

And then there was the fact that Mrs Merrill knew all about his gift (if 'gift' it was) and didn't seem to mind. Indeed, for the first time here was someone who seemed to respect his ability, almost to revere it.

During the first months at the Merrills', Eli experienced a rare peace. He moved there just ahead of a spring that arrived over the Welsh Marches with an uncommonly tender beauty. The sky shone in hyacinth candescence over the white lambs, which tottered into their newborn world, seeming emissaries of promise. Beneath their unsteady hooves, the greening fields glowed in the light as the surrounding hedges and the ditches gleamed with pale yellow celandines. Surely, Eli Faring said to himself as he walked to work one day, this is God's land.

In those days Eli was thinking much about God. He made an oblique overture to the local priest, a man who had trained at Oxford and considered himself intellectually above his parish but with very little vocation for pastoral care. Afraid of the facts of life, he had a corresponding abhorrence of death and the pillars that ran down his face to his mouth grew more pronounced when Eli, very tentatively, raised the subject of his unusual talent. The priest, whose calling commanded that he should help to shepherd human souls out of life, abruptly turned the conversation to the works of Thomas Aquinas.

The name 'Thomas' brought in its wake memories of the friend who had been the subject of the first of Eli's mortal prophecies. It was not a happy association. Eli politely filtered out the earnest vicar's discussions of medieval theology and reverted to the safer wisdoms of the pagan countryside.

Eli's distance from humankind had brought about a corresponding closeness to nature. The natural world, being free of self-consciousness, harboured no fear of death, and thus he hoped, prayed, even, in his own fashion, that he could do it no harm.

And during this period, the former Mrs Lynch seemed hospitality itself. Each evening Eli joined her and Frank for supper at their kitchen table, more a high tea, really: boiled eggs, slices of pink ham, homemade bread, teacakes and strong tea, all comforting reminders of the childhood he had lost. On Sundays Eli got in the way of accompanying his hostess on a walk – not the far-flung kind he made alone, but a pleasant enough ramble over fields that were not too muddy for her shoes – while Frank messed about in the outhouses with the vintage cars that were his passion.

A little more than six months after Eli had moved in, Maureen Merrill said, 'We've got Frank's Aunt Ellen coming for tea this Saturday. It would be nice if you could join us.' If this invitation was unnecessary, since he habitually joined the Merrills for tea, Eli didn't, even inwardly, remark it.

The tea, pork pie, beetroot and salad with salad cream, followed by stewed plums and junket, passed uneventfully. Frank's Aunt Ellen (more a second cousin, it had been explained) was a tiny, shrivelled woman with curvature of the spine. She sat with her face bent over the blue and white plate, on which Maureen had loaded pie and salad, hardly speaking, except to utter quiet platitudes about the weather and the cost of living. But she had, Eli thought, a nice mouth, curving and kindly, which smiled at him, shyly, over the pie and later the stewed plums.

After she had gone, driven home by Frank in one of the not-too-valuable vintage cars, Maureen Merrill said, 'Did you happen to look at Auntie's eyes at all, Eli?'

Not too surprised by this question, for Mrs Merrill was nosy, he answered truthfully that he had.

'See any, you know . . .?'

The purport of the question hung in the air. Eli shook his head and went to his room. That night, he went to the local pub and got drunk on pale ale.

The following morning he was late for breakfast, and, being nearly late for work too, Maureen scolded him, in the manner she had adopted, a gentle scold, like a mother's, she would have said. But instead of responding with his customary sheepish grin, Eli sat over his tea and toast, saying nothing. Maureen assumed it was a hangover from the unaccustomed alcohol and began an equally maternal homily on the perils of drink. But he cut her short, quite savagely, and went off to work without the usual goodbye wave.

That evening he again went down to the Lamb and Stag and came home half plastered, this time on whisky.

The next evening Maureen accosted her lodger.

'Eli, have you got it into your head that we were wanting you to tell us anything about Auntie Ellen because it would help us in any way, you know, to know when . . .?' She shrugged and looked over to Frank as if for help, though everyone in the room was aware that Maureen looked for help from no one.

The young man gazed past the protuberant blue eyes peering into his own. He cast a glance at Frank, who was standing in the doorway, wiping his oily hands on a rag, and his expression softened. 'Nothing to worry about there.'

At the end of the week, when Maureen Merrill went up to 'do' Eli's room, she found it clean and tidy and stripped of all his possessions. There was a note on the bed. *Thanks for all your hospitality. Eliot.*

In the post-Merrill days Eli eschewed human company, making tentative contact only when hunger pressed and funds had run dry. One day, when the wolf seemed crouched on the threshold, he passed a collection of caravans parked by the roadside. A woman sitting on the steps of one of these shouted to him as he passed, 'Tell your fortune, my darling.'

Eli stopped. Used as he was to telling, in a manner of speaking, the fortunes of others, he had never been challenged over his own. The woman, who had a knowing eye, spotted the hesitation.

'Cross my palm with silver?'

'I haven't any money to spare.'

The woman looked at him with shrewd green eyes. 'You a natural?'

'What?'

'A natural. Like me. You see things?'

Eli stared at the ground and made no answer.

'You do, don't you, yeah? Come here, dear, there's honour among thieves they say and ought to be among our kind, yes?'

There is a comfort in being seen. None the less, Eli approached the woman warily, as if she were an animal who might spring and demolish him. But he did as he was told and held out a hand.

'You a southpaw?'

'Left-handed? Yes.'

'Southpaws often have the knack. Let's have a look at you.'

She traced a line in his hand.

'Not a long life but our kind don't live long. You ever been married?'

Eli shook his head.

'I see a child. Pretty girl. A niece maybe?'

'I'm an only child.'

'Lonely that. But there's a child waiting for you along the way. Now then, there's money here if you want it.'

'Money?'

'In your line. If you want it. The hand only tells what's possible. It's up to us whether we make it stick or not. Let's have a look at love. Got a girlfriend?'

Eli coloured. 'No.'

The woman's knowing eyes raked him up and down. 'Nice big fellow like you.'

'I'd better get going.'

'You want to come along with us? It's not regular money but there's enough and there's company.' Her hand slid up his back. He felt the pressure of strong fingers on his lumbar spine. 'We all need company, darling.'

Eli was a virgin. The woman with her hard lean limbs, though undoubtedly his elder by a decade at least, was not unattractive.

'Okay.'

'That's right. I'm Della. Delilah to those in the know. My mum was a church-going feminist. She liked it when the women won. And you're . . .'

He hesitated, wondering whether to try for a new name. New start, new name. But nothing came to him. 'I'm Eli,' Eli said.

*

For the next two years Eli travelled with Della in her caravan. The ragged little troop was not true Romany, but there was, as Della said, Romany blood in there somewhere. She and her brother Tony had a grand-mother who was rumoured to have come from distant Romany stock. Together the brother and sister worked fairs: Della was the palmist and mystic globe reader, Tony ran the Pop the Duck gallery, and fat Jeff and little Pauline, when they travelled with them, the Bouncy House of Horror.

For a while Eli was simply regarded as Della's man – useful for repairing the vans, inflating the Bouncy House and fixing its occasional punctures, acting as general dogsbody and, as Tony put it, 'Seeing our Della's okay.'

And the sex was a comfort. Della was kind in bed, perhaps to compensate for a marked unkindness out of it. Out of it, she upbraided Eli for clumsiness, inexperi-ence and what she called 'nancy-boy' weaknesses; but at night she was tolerant of his diffidence, even generous. There was something reassuring in her well-muscled body and her hard-soled feet, which rasped his flesh as she lodged them above his hipbones.

She gave him other things too. Material things, lifted from various department stores. His favourite was a washbag printed with images of Donald Duck.

For reasons unfathomed, despite her earlier sugges-tion of potential financial reward, Della was tactful about Eli's 'gift', never inquiring too much into what it was or how he might use it. Until one day she said, idly, 'Tony's got a new fan. Take a look at him when you have a chance, darling.'

Tony's 'fans' were eclectic. Some were underage girls, often with tattoos like rashes on their bare arms; others were male and middle aged, or elderly, as was the case with this one, a portly man whose stomach cascaded in rolls into his too-short trousers. He was called, most unsuitably, for his manner was far from imperial, Rex.

Rex wore shirts patterned with bright tropical birds and sported an earring, which added no element of jauntiness to his pale, jowelled face.

'What you want me to look for?' Eli asked, as if he didn't know.

'Oh, whatever you see.'

'He got money?'

For once Della misread him. 'Tony reckons. A big house, anyway, and no relatives to leave it to.'

'I'll take a look next time.'

'Next time' was a barbecue where Tony cooked chicken wings, handing them round swathed in red paper napkins to stave off the barbecue sauce. Rex sat on an oil drum on which he beat out the rhythms of the music, making a fairground of the balmy evening from the portable CD player, his sausage fingers thrumming to indicate a familiarity with the tune, which it was evident he didn't possess. Evident anyway to Eli.

Later, lifting herself from Eli's prone body, Della

asked, with an unusual casualness, 'See anything in our Tony's Rex, honey?' 'Honey' was a term she used when she wanted more of him than usual.

'Nothing,' said Eli, and turned over.

He left the next day, while Della was at the bank, leaving behind the Donald Duck washbag.

After this, life grew harder for Eli. Della had taken care of him in her way. Left to his own devices he was at a loss. He survived hand-to-mouth, eking out a living doing menial jobs where he could; but in his terror of his gift he could no longer look anyone straight in the eye, which gave him a shifty expression that didn't inspire trust.

One evening he hitched a lift with a landscape gardener on his way to a job on a Lincolnshire country estate. The gardener was one of those gregarious men who like to be of service. Recognizing a fellow being in a parlous condition, he told Eli that the estate was often short of workers and suggested he could put in a word for him with the manager. As luck would have it, the estate manager needed more men for the coming pheasant shoots, and, observing that he'd got a worker on his hands, one he could rely on, asked Eli to stay on when the season was over.

Eli was put to work on rough labouring jobs in the woods and kitchen gardens. The post came with some basic accommodation, a converted outhouse on the estate, and although the wages were pitiful there were perks: produce was thrown in, vegetables and eggs and all the firewood he needed. The electrics ran off the meters in the big house, so there were few expenses to meet. For the first time in years, amid grass and leaves and birds and people who were by and large indifferent to him, Eli felt something like happiness.

One day, walking in the woods, he met a young boy, the grandson of the owners of the house. The boy was a late child of a late marriage, and his birth, as such births often are, was felt as something of a miracle – a godsend, anyway. The boy, an only child, was bored and maybe a little lonely. He took to visiting Eli in his shabby home whenever he came to visit his grandparents. One evening, when Eli was showing him how to carve and was crouched down with his arms round the boy's shoulders to guide the knife he had lent him, the boy's mother burst in, snatched at her son and hurried him out, shooting a threatening backward glance at Eli as she went.

Three days later he was given his notice.

'Been told to cut down on extra staff, I'm sorry,' the estate manager said, not meeting Eli's eyes. 'Last in first out it is, see.'

He was a decent man and sent Eli off with his next month's pay and some old tools for which the estate had duplicates.

*

By the time he had turned sixty, Eli was a pretty well-hardened vagrant. He walked the roads, sticking to Wales, which he felt was closer to a home than anywhere else, seeking occasional employment mending small household items and, during the warmer months, sleeping rough outside. Often he chatted aloud, ignoring the looks he prompted. Sometimes he chatted to his mother or to his gran.

Once, recalling a holiday as a child with his gran in Bexhill, he made his way circuitously down to an unfashionable seaside resort near Aberdovey. It was out of season and there were only a handful of people on the windy esplanade to patronize the slot-machine arcades. He walked past these, and the trashy shops selling plastic buckets and spades, and down some concrete steps, festooned with dampish bladder-wrack, on to the pebbly sand. The tide was out, and he took off his shoes and walked towards the far-away margin of the sea.

The sand grew wetter and began to fill his footprints, till he reached the water itself and stood bearing the sharp cold of its salt bracelets around his ankles with something akin to pleasure.

A poem, memorized long ago at the school where Mr Lynch had taught, half came to his mind.

It was towards evening and the first star was puncturing the greening sky. As he stood observing the splinter of light let through by the star, he imagined a tremendous bank of light feeding it, beyond the visible sky. A light where he would feel at home, maybe, at last. Twisting stiffly round, he saw that a wobbly string of multicoloured lights had come on, decking the esplanade, and, turning outward again, he observed the few gold lights of small fishing craft dusting the horizon. The immenseness of the sea unrolled before him as the green and rose sky bled into the bruised violet-blue of its waters. A wave broke over his shins and drew back, sucking his feet down into the fine stones with a hiss, and a few uncertain lines of the long-forgotten poem filtered back.

> . . . the grating roar
> Of pebbles which the waves draw back
> . . . and bring
> The eternal note of sadness in.

All of a sudden an acute sense of the terrible beauty of the world flooded through him and he felt mortally afraid. Unused to such fear in himself – though all too familiar with it in others – he hurried back up the unpeopled beach, panting now, to collect his shoes and made his way, still barefoot, to the bus shelter, where he caught a bus to the nearest village.

Thereafter he stayed inland.

As more years passed it became only the winters that he dreaded. One bitterly cold late February afternoon he came to a run-down, out-of-the-way hamlet. At its outskirts, he found a few surviving walls, the remnants of an old chapel, with an ancient yew tree growing close by. He had with him his sleeping bag, his waterproof tarpaulin, a supply of biscuits, the heel of a cheese and two cans of beer. He was tired and near perished; his feet were frozen and hurt him. The aged tree looked a fair-enough shelter for an ageing man.

He had eaten some biscuits, a portion of cheese and drunk the cans of beer, wrapped himself up and laid his head on a knot of root covered with a sack, when a touch on his shoulder disturbed him.

A child. A girl child, slight, with fair hair, was standing looking him over.

'Come quickly,' she said. 'Please, mister. It's my gran.'

Eli hauled himself up off the ground with difficulty and followed after the girl, stumbling a little, for his feet were numb and his knees stiff, to a stone cottage, set back from the road alongside the ruined chapel. The odd little creature pushed open the door of the cottage and hurried inside.

It was dark as they crossed the threshold but to Eli's frozen limbs it felt wonderfully warm, a warmth which emanated, he could see, from a coal fire in what he presumed was the parlour. The girl, however, did not stop but took him up some stairs and into a bedroom.

'Here,' she said, 'I brought him. I brought the man you said was here.'

Eli gazed at a bed in which an old woman lay, her head covered in a grubby, once white, woollen baby's shawl. Her papery eyelids were closed, but as Eli

approached, shoved forward by the little girl with a violence that seemed disproportionate to her size, the old
woman opened her eyes and looked into his. The eyes, a
bright blue, were surpassingly clear for a woman of, he
would guess, well over eighty years.

But the voice, when she spoke, sounded to his ear as
old as time. 'You have the gift.'

Eli, gazing into her eyes, saw something unusual. An
image. A tiny image of a boy. Surely it was . . .? But the
papery lids quivered and closed again.

The girl pulled at his sleeve. 'You can go downstairs
now.'

Obedient to his small summoner, Eli descended and,
not knowing what he should do, went into the fire-lit
parlour. It was certainly very snug. Whatever they
wanted of him, he was glad to be detained even a little
while from the heartless February night.

Eli sat down in one of the floral-covered armchairs
and looked into the blue and coral flames licking the
coals. The image of the boy he had seen in the old woman's eyes came back to him. All at once, he recognized it:
an image of himself before . . . before the gift that had
cursed his life was known, to himself – or to anyone. If
only he could go back to that time. 'If wishes were
horses beggars would ride', his gran had used to say. His
poor gran, sent away because of him. Thank God that
was one death he had not been there to foresee.

After some time he heard the girl come down the

stairs. He felt rather than heard her enter the parlour. She spoke close to his ear and her voice was soft.

'It's mortal chill out there. Will you take a drink before you go?'

So, now I am supposed to go, thought Eli. He wouldn't mind staying here, with the fire and the old lady and the odd child. And the thought of his own lost gran.

A profound love for his grandmother welled up inside him. She knew me, he thought to himself. She knew. And he recalled a certain look in her watery blue eyes.

Aloud he said, 'I should be on my way.'

'Ah, not yet,' said the girl. 'Take a drop before I see you out.'

It was generally agreed that that February night was so cold – eleven below freezing, they said – it was hardly surprising that a vagrant had died in his sleep, on the ground, within the remains of the old chapel. Nothing could be found among his effects to identify him, though it is true not much effort was made.

A local woman, a recluse, also with no known relatives, had died in a neighbouring cottage the same night. But a letter of wishes was found, with money for her funeral, requesting that any person in the parish dying the same night as she did be buried beside her in the churchyard.

There were no dissenters to this suggestion. And the

only mourners at the joint funeral were a young couple, merely passing by, they said, with their daughter, a pretty, fair-haired child who had, the parish priest observed later to his wife, remarkable blue eyes.

Rescue

'Of course death is exciting,' Verity Lichfield pronounced. She helped herself to another cucumber sandwich. A table had been laid by Desmond Davies's sister for those who had come to condole for the sudden, and shocking, death of his wife, Rosa.

'But it's awful.' Her companion, Eleanor Bishop, tried, not for the first time, to repress the thought that Verity's name had apparently committed her to a life's mission of making challenging observations. Not succeeding, she inquired, 'What makes you say that?'

'Look around you.' Verity was vetting the plate of sandwiches, searching past the egg and ham for more cucumber on white. She had been, given the circumstances, tactlessly vocal, Eleanor thought, about 'the health squad's obsession' with brown bread. Thwarted in her quest for cucumber, Verity fell back on the less substantial nourishment of causing disturbance.

'People lead such dull lives that a spot of drama is thrilling. All that opportunity for bogus emotion and equally bogus recollections and then the fun of rewriting history. And, apart from the novelty value' – she paused, having detected a cucumber sandwich concealed beneath a tuna mayonnaise – 'there's the thrill that they have so narrowly missed death themselves.'

'Schadenfreude, you mean?'

'If you must.' Among Verity's more annoying affectations, in Eleanor's view, was a refusal to use foreign terms however embedded in common English speech. 'I would simply call it the pleasure of a close shave. A dice with death is a wonderful tonic to the spirits.' She turned smiling, showing perfect white teeth.

How can she have kept them so white? Eleanor wondered. She was the same age as Verity, almost a year younger, in fact, and her own teeth were showing the stained yellow of age. It seemed unlikely that Verity would have gone in for what she would surely dismiss as the 'modern obsession' with whitening.

As if to emphasize the superior whiteness of her teeth, Verity yawned. 'For myself, I find death very tiring.'

It also makes you greedy, Eleanor thought, watching Verity's large freckled hand work forensically through the remaining sandwiches. Having failed in her search, she started on a bowl of Twiglets.

'I remember these,' she said. 'D'you remember? We always had them at parties. And sausages on toothpicks stuck in grapefruit.'

Why was it that grapefruit featured so often in medical images? Eleanor wondered. 'Was it really grapefruit?' Her mind flew back to the days when the three of them had worn party frocks with wide sashes and Alice bands in their hair. She, Verity and Rosa were all the children of committed socialists – Rosa named for Rosa Luxemburg and herself for Marx's daughter. Their parents had been comrades in their student days and the youthful connection had held over time. The three girls had grown up together, stayed at each other's houses so regularly that their parents had become virtually interchangeable, gone on peace marches together, camped in out-of-the-way, sometimes dangerous places. In more recent years they had supported each other when one by one their parents, whose care they had parcelled out to each other in much the same way that food had been parcelled out on the communal holidays, had fallen like ripe fruit off the tree of life to return to the earth, since there was never any question with them of any ethereal afterlife.

There were other children. But the three eldest girls, all born within a year, had remained the closest. And now Rosa had left them betimes. Never would Eleanor have predicted that Rosa would go first. She was so full of life. She smiled, realizing how Verity would scoff at such clichés.

'What are you grinning about?'

'I was thinking how she'd have enjoyed all the fuss and to-do.'

This, while not a strictly truthful answer to the question, would indubitably have been true of their departed friend.

'She'd have loved it,' Verity surprisingly – for in general she considered psychological observation to be strictly her own preserve – agreed. 'All those people who barely knew her, weeping and wailing and rending their garments.'

'And the stories,' Eleanor prompted, grateful to have been left off the hook, for Verity's tongue was as sharp as ever. Maybe more so; less constrained by the natural benevolence of youth. 'All slightly embroidered to put themselves in a good light.'

She herself was not immune from this deception. She was recalling now how she had exaggerated the last conversation she had had with Rosa. The exchange had been a brief and businesslike consulting of diaries to sort out dates when they or their husbands were away or they might meet; not at all the right tone for their last conversation. But how could she, or anyone, have known?

The words of a hymn floated inward. 'And live each day as if the last.' Was that George Herbert? Soon she would have to consider what hymns should be sung at Rosa's funeral, for, with the predictable reaction of an eldest born, Rosa had set her face against her parents' atheism and embraced Christianity.

Eleanor herself, though more tamely, since everything she did was in a lower key than Rosa's, had followed her in this. Only Verity, the single one of the three girls named not for a socialist icon but after a religious aunt, had held fast to the unfaith of their parents.

As if reading her mind, Verity remarked, 'I suppose we'll have to sort out the service.'

'I don't think Desmond will be up to it.'

'Desmond!' It was daunting how fierce Verity could be.

'He's dreadfully cut up.'

'He's sorry for himself, that's all. And he's too self-obsessed to think about what she'd have wanted. No, it's down to us. Or rather down to you. I haven't a clue what she'd have wanted from the God department.'

'"Awake, My Soul, and with the Sun",' Eleanor quoted suddenly.

'What?'

'It's a hymn. I've been trying to remember where a line from it came.'

'What was the line?'

Eleanor, certain her friend asked only to mock, said defensively, '"And live each day as if our last."'

Perversely, Verity chose to approve. 'Unusually sensible for a hymn. Are you going to suggest that?'

'I don't know,' Eleanor said. 'I don't think so. I think she'd want Herbert and Bunyan.'

'And Blake?'

'I don't know. I think maybe it's too –'

'Tired?'

'I somehow associate "Jerusalem" nowadays with rugby. But Desmond may want it and we can hardly veto his choice. He's very cut up,' she said again.

'He just can't think how he's going to cope without her,' Verity said pitiless. 'It's all about him.' She paused to note further examples of crocodile tears and histrionics among some newcomers who had come to condole. 'I do wish Rosie were here to see all this. She'd simply roar with laughter.'

'How strange,' Eleanor said. 'I've not heard you call her that for years.'

It was at the camp in the New Forest, where the families went for Whitsun, and they were playing hanky rescue. She'd never met anyone since who had played this game so maybe they'd made it up. One person was 'It' while the others hid. Once seen, you could be sent 'home' to a chosen point, a tree or bush, but from there you could be rescued by the sighting of a wave of a handkerchief. The art lay in concealing yourself in the right position to free the captives; positions that, among the adventurous older children, usually involved perilous tree climbs.

The game depended on honourable behaviour. You mayn't escape until you truly saw the wave of a hanky. It was interesting, Eleanor mused, that no one ever seemed to cheat. Would that be so nowadays? she wondered.

One game in particular came to mind. Verity had been It and Rosa had found a particularly cunning place to hide in the crotch of a vast oak. Her discreet waves had set any number of prisoners free, and when she was finally caught Verity had said, admiringly, 'Rosie, you must have dryad blood in your veins. I looked up there a million times and couldn't see you for the leaves.'

And Rosa had looked at Verity with her slightly slanted grey-green eyes so that she did indeed appear for a moment quite otherworldly.

That summer, when the three families had gone to Scotland, to stay in 'yet another bloody damp house', as Eleanor's brother Tom put it, Eleanor had felt a little out of it. Verity and Rosa seemed to have a special understanding, and, though they apparently included her in everything as much as ever, she felt subtly excluded in a way that hurt and she didn't comprehend. The feeling had passed but hearing Verity use her old childhood name for their friend brought it back. Then, that's right, they had quarrelled, Verity and Rosa. Having appeared so close that summer, the next summer they had each turned to her, as if she were the special one and the other was cold-shouldered. Hardly realizing what she was saying, she asked, 'Why did you and Rosa quarrel?'

'Quarrel?' Verity was scowling. She had thickened out over the years. Her once lean body was now burly, and she sat with her knees planted apart, as women do when they have given up hope of sex.

'That summer after Galloway. The time we were in Wales, in Laugharne. You and Rosa weren't speaking, or something. Something, anyway, was wrong. You must remember it.'

Verity's face flushed dark red. 'I haven't a clue what you're on about.'

She was in love with Rosa, Eleanor realized with a start. Of course that would explain it. The sly looks between the two of them, the unexpected closeness that had shut her out and then the following summer the strange coldness. But that was long ago. They had made it up since. Of course they had. The three of them had so often been together through the years. No one knew any one of them as thoroughly as they knew each other.

Verity was getting to her feet, struggling a little to haul her weight up from the chair, and for the first time Eleanor saw she was to be pitied. Rosa's Desmond was a poor fish but Verity had married a truly vile man, who had taken off not only with a younger woman but also with most of Verity's money. Money which, ironically, had come from the religious aunt from whom she had also had her name.

I'm the lucky one, Eleanor thought. I have Tony. Thinking this, she wasn't surprised to see him across the room.

'There you are,' he said, and as always she took heart from the look in his eyes, a look she knew was hers alone. 'And Verity too. How are you, my dear?'

'As you'd expect.' Stiffly, Verity allowed herself to be kissed. She gave the impression, Eleanor noted, of conferring a favour by allowing Tony briefly to hold her. But he wouldn't mind. He would laugh and say, 'Poor old thing' because that, Eleanor perceived with a pang, was what Verity had become.

Perhaps she never got over Rosa, Eleanor conjectured. I wouldn't be surprised. Rosa was extraordinary, and how odd that I never saw what she was to Verity before today. But death does that, I suppose. Makes you see things differently. Or for the first time.

'Shall we go?' Tony asked, his hand uxoriously – delightfully so – on the crook of her elbow. 'Have you had enough, darling?'

She had and was grateful to him. But 'Verity?' she mouthed. 'Should we . . .?'

He shrugged, implying whatever she chose to do was fine by him.

'Verity, we're going. Would you like a lift? Or maybe come back –'

'Thanks, no.' The response, Eleanor thought, was needlessly brusque. 'I'll ring for a cab.' She kissed Eleanor and passed a cheek swiftly past Tony's.

As they said goodbye to Desmond, he laid his hand on Eleanor's arm. 'Stay in touch, please, because I'll need your help with the funeral. Oh, and there are some drawings of hers you might like and I'd like you to see.'

The Chapel of Rest was clinically white, the wood all light and the soft furnishings a municipal blue.

'You'd better take this,' Tony said, offering his handkerchief to Eleanor.

'I wish she wasn't being burned.'

'She's dead. She won't care.'

'Tony! Don't be so . . .' she faded.

'What?'

'I don't know. So bloody pragmatic.'

As she'd predicted, Desmond had chosen 'Jerusalem' for the funeral.

'It's both religious and radical,' he explained, kissing Eleanor. 'She'd have wanted that.'

How swift people were to appropriate the taste of the departed. Eleanor was by no means sure Rosa would have wanted 'Jerusalem' to send her off. She was always original. How awful that Blake of all people should have become an institution. Eleanor comforted herself that Tony was, perhaps, right. Even in any after-life it was unlikely one cared too much about such things. Rosa and Blake had joined the ranks of the mute, and life and the living would always have the stronger voice.

The wake after the funeral was held in Rosa's studio, which was not part of their Chiswick house but one of a set of studios near the crematorium, towards Kew. Both house and studio had been acquired before the areas became fashionable.

'Old Desmond'll sell this for a tidy sum,' Tony said as they entered. 'He'll be quids in.'

'Shut up, he'll hear you.'

'I bet he's secretly quite chuffed she's died.'

'Tony, stop it!'

The studio was undeniably a good choice of venue. A large space, free of furniture, making it easy to mill and chat. And besides there were Rosa's paintings and drawings, some still in progress, hanging round the walls so that her presence was visibly with them.

People talked animatedly of how her reputation as an artist had grown so much in recent years and how her fortunes had prospered accordingly. Unkind souls suggested, in lowered tones, that this was just as well, as Desmond had never been much of an earner.

'What's he currently doing?' a man with a wispy Van Dyck beard, whose face Eleanor recognized but whose name escaped her, asked.

'He's got some sort of admin post at the Royal College.'

'Can only have been through her influence!' was the scornful rejoinder.

Death makes people savage, she reflected. I suppose it's a way of venting other feelings; or maybe an assertion of being alive. Anger, as she was sure Verity would say, is vivifying.

Eleanor, looking around for Verity, saw Desmond appear instead with a glass of red wine held at a dangerous angle.

'Desmond, your wine. Mind your shirt.' The shirt, she noted, was already stained and had a button half off. Quite possibly this was deliberate. He was one of those men whose being seemed to demand that one take responsibility for him.

Desmond took a remedial swig of wine. 'I wanted to show you her drawings. Come over here.' Lurching slightly, he led Eleanor to a table where a large artist's portfolio lay open. 'Here, see this one. That's you, isn't it?'

A drawing of her youthful face looked innocently out at her. Goodness, I was pretty then, she thought.

'And this is Verity, isn't it?'

Verity, looking quite lovely, her hands, utterly untoad-like, raking with careless grace through dark, dishevelled hair. And here was Rosa herself, quite a recent self-portrait, beautiful still with her slant cat's eyes and archaic smile.

'Do look at them,' Desmond said. 'I've not trawled through them all yet' – how like him to say 'trawled', Eleanor thought – 'but everyone she really loved seems to be here.'

And it was true, Eleanor reflected. For Rosa had been drawing all her life. She had always been the artist. At one time it seemed as if Verity would be the writer, but after one decently reviewed novel nothing had come of that; while she, Eleanor, had been the musical one. But she was merely a badly paid music teacher now. Neither she nor Verity had turned out to have Rosa's talent.

But the drawings – oh the pity of it – were quite mar-vellous. Each of the faces she knew so well, herself and

Verity, her own brothers, Tom and Ian, Verity's sister
Anna, Rosa's brother, Charles, who had gone to Aus-
tralia and obviously wasn't planning to come back, even
for his sister's death, and her sister Kate, who had turned
Tory and mortified their parents. Thinking of this, it
struck her that Kate wasn't there – and then she remembered that Kate had written to say that her husband was
undergoing open heart surgery and that in the circumstances she felt she'd better stay at his side.

All the parents were there too, growing touchingly
older as she turned over the sheets of paper, as if turning the pages in some Book of Life. Now here was
Desmond with his and Rosa's children, Harry and Char-
lotte, and her and Tony's children, Angus, Beth and
Alexandra. Studying the portraits, Eleanor could discern
a special feeling towards each of the subjects. She did
love us, she thought.

At the back of the portfolio was a pocket with a flap
tucked in, and, opening it, curiously, she found another
sheaf of drawings, smaller than the others but on first
impression the execution struck her as more careful.

With a sharp shock down her breastbone she recognized a face. No, many faces. The many faces of Tony:
Tony still quite young, Tony with a beard – from when?
Ten years ago, it must have been – Tony aged but still
undeniably handsome.

At the bottom of one of the portraits a date was pen-
cilled. Last year's date – last July's date, to be precise, a

date that Eleanor knew with a sudden awful clarity was exactly when Tony was away last summer in Madrid. 'At a conference,' he had said, kissing her. 'Not for you, darling. I'll have no time off for jaunts.'

She stood holding the drawing before her while the eyes she knew so intimately regarded her with that special look she had supposed hers alone. Behind her, she felt the same eyes knifing into her back. Wordlessly, she turned to him.

'It was over,' he said. 'Honestly, that was the last time.'

Furiously, she hissed, 'How could you? You hardly showed a shred of emotion when she died. Or now. How could you? How could you be so horribly fucking, *disgustingly* cool?' For suddenly, weirdly, it was for Rosa she minded.

Behind Tony, Verity was standing with an expression which told her, incontrovertibly, that Verity had known. Of course she had. She had loved Rosa too. And she saw things with that terrible veracity that mirrored her name. But for once – and Eleanor was not yet to know whether this was something she was glad of – the passion for truth-telling had been withheld. Only she, Eleanor, had been in ignorance, left out, excluded, as in the old days.

Weeping angrily, she strode past the two of them, reaching for Tony's handkerchief, which was powerless to rescue her from the prison of this new knowledge.

A Sad Tale

———◀◉▶———

(for Rowan)

The boy knew there was something wrong. He always knew at once when anything was not altogether right with his mother, but on this occasion it was an unnerving sense that with his father things were not as they should be. He knew his father less instinctively than he knew his mother. But then he saw less of his father, since his father's position meant that he had important matters of state to attend to, more important than the state of an eight-year-old boy. And, while his uncle had been staying (he wasn't his uncle by blood but his father and he had been brought up together so were as close as brothers), his father had been more than usually occupied. The two old friends had gone off hunting together, had visited further parts of the country and all manner of junketing had been organized and seemingly enjoyed. But now his uncle was preparing to leave.

There had been a small informal dinner on the last evening of his uncle's stay, which the boy had been permitted to attend. At the end of it, as he was saying goodnight to his parents and their guest, his father had taken him by his shoulders and squeezed his nose, which had hurt, though it was apparently done in fun, and then peered into his eyes and asked him if he thought they, that is the two of them, were alike.

They were alike, he knew. As like as two eggs, his mother's women said, though he didn't take too much account of them. They liked to pet and caress him as if he were still a baby, and he really only cared for that sort of thing when it was his mother kissing him. He had told his father just the other day that he liked to fight but he had merely said so to please. He liked to please his father. But, in truth, he far preferred his mother's gentler ways and hoped that it was she whom he truly took after. She was always kind and funny and loved to play and joke with him and have him tell her stories. She liked his stories better than anyone's and he knew that she didn't fib or pretend in saying so, as older people often did, always with the knowing faces that betrayed their real thoughts. No, she sincerely loved to hear his inventions and praised them in a manner that lifted his heart and made him want to better them for her. He often lay in bed at night, for he was usually sent to bed long before sleep overtook him, or in the mornings when he woke early, and knew he'd be in trouble if he rose too soon, making up brave new worlds for her in his head.

He had lain awake that night, with his father's wine-smelling breath still in his nostrils and wondered. And he had woken more than usually early that morning and had lain in bed, happy to do so because a sharp frost was in the air and his own breath came cloudy before his face. His greyhound, Dash, sentinel by his bed, opened a golden eye and looked at him inquiringly, but even he seemed to wish to join the rest of the household and returned to houndish sleep.

He leant down and stroked the knobbles on the long canine spine, running his hands along the smooth grey coat to pat the dog's flank. 'Good boy, Dash.' Then he stretched himself out, like a snake uncoiling, as his mother once phrased it, and lay back with one hand behind his head. Outside, he heard the solitary caw of a passing rook or crow and the yap of one of the household hounds, which were not privileged to sleep indoors. And then all around there was quiet.

He loved this dawn quiet. He liked to lie in it as if within his mother's arms, and in its bountiful protection his mind would roam. That morning he found himself thinking about the new world that was about to arrive in the shape of a new brother or sister. His mother had grown to a 'goodly bulk', one of her women pronounced only yesterday. She had been tired lately and less willing to play with him and perhaps, though he didn't quite own this to himself, he had wanted her to play more than usual, as, with a baby coming, he understood that soon she would be more occupied.

He knew that whatever happened he was her boy, her precious one. But the women had begun to mock and tease him about the changes ahead.

'You'll be wanting our company soon enough,' one had said when he pushed her endearments away. 'When your little brother or sister arrives.' He'd turned aside then, afraid that his face might appear to betray a jealousy he frankly didn't feel.

Thinking of this now, he suddenly saw his father's face as he had seen it at dinner the evening before. His father had been talking to his 'uncle', asking his uncle about his own son whom he had left behind in his own country, and his father had called him over and ruffled his hair and asked him that odd question. And then his father had dismissed him and, looking up, he had seen his father stare across the table at his uncle with a strange expression on his face, which he altered to a too-broad smile the moment his uncle looked round.

His uncle had been with them nine months, which seemed a long time to be away from his own family. But that was how it was when people of his father and mother's distinction travelled. Visits abroad seemingly lasted for ever.

He'd heard his father arguing with his uncle, urging him to stay a little longer, which seemed unnecessary, considering how long he'd been a visitor with them already. His uncle had laughed and said really he had to be away, he had duties to attend to and his own dear son would be missing him. And then his father had begged his mother to make the same request and his mother had taken his uncle's arm and walked with him down through the long hall, where the musicians played in the gallery above, and he had seen her squeeze his uncle's arm and then laugh with that soft sweet laugh that was so familiar to him and punch his uncle jestingly on the chest as she sometimes did to his father when she thought he was taking on about something needlessly. And he had also seen his father observe this, staring after the pair of them as they walked so close, her hand linked through their guest's arm.

He's jealous, the boy thought with a sudden lurch to his stomach. The recognition made him feel very alone.

He was aware, from the sly hints dropped and the not so subtle innuendos, that jealousy was what he was expected to feel for his new baby brother or sister. But he had never felt it yet. Now he experienced it as a searing pain near his heart, as if he stood in his father's place and felt with his father's blood beating in his ears.

Was that why his father had asked if they were alike? So he could feel with his father's troubled mind?

He tried to turn his thoughts away to the story he was creating. There was a man he could see in his mind. He wanted to make this a happy story for his mother, for her to take to the childbed with her. But all he could see was an image of a sad-faced man, a man who was haunted by harrowing sprites and vicious goblins.

He didn't want to tell her a sad tale.

Later, dressed and breakfasted and having taken Dash out for his morning run, he went to his mother's room to find her.

He had run to her earlier that morning, after his uncomfortable thoughts in bed, but she had been irritable and brushed him away. She was rarely irritable, especially not with him. It must be that the baby was near to being born.

He walked up the great stairs, praying that he was not too late and that the baby had not begun to arrive already, and along to his mother's room, where he softly opened the door.

And there she was, like a great rose, open and blooming, the baby still in her belly, sitting among her women sewing a tiny silken garment. But, seeing him, she tossed aside her sewing and opened her arms. 'Mamillius, my poppet. Come and amuse me.'

He ran over to her, filled with joy at his return to grace. Hugging her tight, he smelt the peculiar scent of her skin, which reminded him of apricots.

'How shall I?'

'Tell me one of your stories.'

'Sad or merry, would you like?'

'Whatever my clever son has dreamt up for me.'

She was looking at him with her dark grey eyes and

the love and pride he saw there prompted a corresponding love and pride in him.

'A sad tale's best for winter.'

Why on earth had he said that? With all his heart he
had intended to tell her a happy story.

'So be it. And when summer comes you can tell us a
cheerful one. Tell on, my dear muse . . .'

She leaned back on the long settle, pulling him close
to her rounded bosom.

He tried again for a happy image, but the man in his
mind would not be banished. Very well. He would follow where this man was leading. He'd skill enough, he
felt confident, to bring any story, however sad, round to
a happy end.

Edging still closer to his mother, he said, 'I'll tell it in
your ear softly. This is a tale just for you.

'There was a man dwelt by the churchyard –'

As he spoke the words the door was pushed open
and a group of men entered with his father, his face pale
as death, at their head.

One of the women screamed, 'The gods save us!' and
the room went suddenly quiet.

'Take the boy away!'

'No!'

He had cried out and stiffened all his limbs even
before he was conscious of speaking. Around him all
the women remained like statues, stilled.

'Whatever is the matter, Leon?' His mother had risen

and was levelling her cool gaze at his father, but she used her pet name for him: 'Leon', or sometimes 'Leo', for his father was born under that sign.

'I said *take the boy away*! I will not have him near her.'

A man, one he'd never liked because he had once kicked Dash, moved towards him and in reaction he moved still closer to his mother, so that he could feel the quickened rise and fall of her breathing through her birthing stays.

'Mamillius. Leave us, sir.'

'I will not, Father.'

The man glanced at his father, who gave a nod, and the boy felt his right wrist caught in a burning grip.

'Let me go!'

'Let him go.' His mother's voice, unafraid, authoritative, coldly commanding. The man loosened his grip and stood back.

His mother looked down at him. Then she bent and placed the palm of her hand delicately against his cheek. On her own cheeks a hectic red was dancing, belying the coolness of her tone. 'Do as your father asks, Mamillius. We'll go on with the story later. I shall look forward to it.'

He hesitated, not wanting to leave her. Not wanting to leave her for his own sake but also for her sake too, because he was suddenly, and dreadfully, afraid.

'I don't want to.'

'You go, chick. Go and play and I'll come and find you soon.'

'Promise?'

A laugh like a fox's bark exploded into the hushed room. 'A promise from a whore? For that is what your mother is, my son. Leave her with the child in her womb that is –'

'No!' He spun round to meet the livid features of his father. He knew very well what a 'whore' was. A bad woman. A vile woman. A woman without honour.

'Mamillius, sweetness, please leave us.'

His mother was the daughter of the Emperor of Russia and she never cried, but the look in her eyes was now so full of grief that his own filled with sharp responsive tears.

'Mother?'

'Mamillius, my own love, for my sake please go.'

He could not refuse this plea and so fled from the room and saw nothing of her, or anyone, for most of that day.

There were raised voices and comings and goings and no one came to care for him or to see that he was fed. Unused to a neglect he had often longed for, he went down to the kitchens to forage for food. The kitchen staff stopped what they were saying when they saw him there. There was a moment of awkwardness, a distinct unease, and then one of cooks came forward with a smile and a cold pastie and some small beer and invited him to stay and eat at the kitchen table. He was grateful for their company.

Very late that night, as he lay unable to sleep, still fully clothed, his Aunt Paulina came to his room.

He didn't much like Aunt Paulina, although she was his mother's best friend (not an actual aunt any more than 'Uncle' Polixenes was really an uncle), but he knew that she was good. 'Good as a purge for the bowels is good,' his father had remarked once, and his mother had cuffed him playfully.

Aunt Paulina was tall, like his mother, but there the similarity ended. She was bone thin and her face was a mass of creased leather lines like those on the old bindings in his father's library. Her hands were long and bony too and her nails yellow and not always clean. Her tongue was notoriously sharp, but there was no sharpness in her tone when she spoke now.

'Mamillius, child.'

'Where is my mother?'

His aunt looked bothered. She was, he knew, a truthful woman and he could tell she was struggling to speak honestly to him.

'She has been detained.'

'Detained? Where? Why?'

Again, his aunt hesitated. 'They, your parents, have matters to attend to. Meanwhile your mother would wish you to rest.'

'Can I see her?'

'Maybe later, Mamillius.'

He was obliged to obey. Powerful as he might one day be, he was still a mere eight-year-old child. There was only so much he could ask, or challenge. Unwillingly, he changed into his nightgown, resenting his aunt's continued presence as he did so, and climbed with the appearance of obedience into bed.

'Will I read to you?'

He was not a baby that he needed to be read to. 'No, thank you, Aunt.'

'I'll stay awhile until you sleep.'

But he did not sleep. He lay with his eyes shut, breathing deeply, until he felt Paulina bend down to listen to him and kiss him, which itself was disturbing as her cheeks felt bristly and she wasn't the kissing kind, then move quietly to the door.

He waited long enough to be sure she had descended the stairs and then rose again, pulling on breeches into which he tucked his nightgown. With night fallen it was colder still, so he put on the bearskin waistcoat which Uncle Polixenes had brought as a gift for him when he arrived from Bohemia.

The dormant hound began to struggle loyally to his feet but he whispered, 'Lie down, Dash. Sleep, boy.'

Then, carrying in his hand his soft leather boots, he went quietly from the room.

Light refracting from the candle-lit sconces in the hall below brought the long stretches of the upper corridors dimly into view. He doubted that his mother was still in her room, but he made his way there, up the second staircase, through the tapestry-wadded silence to be sure. Nothing but the tiny silk frock she had been making for the baby flung on to the long settle gave any sign of her recent presence. She must have left the room in a hurry. She was nothing if not tidy, his mother. He picked up the morsel of soft fabric and pressed it to his face, smelling the familiar apricot scent of his mother's skin.

Where had she gone? And what had occurred to bring about that awful accusation? There could be no truth in it. His father must have been misled, told a tale by some villain. Was it Uncle Polixenes?

As he stood there in the half-dark, holding the unborn baby's dress, he heard a wild voice from below.

'I tell you by all that's holy the child is Polixenes'.'

And following that another voice, also raised but this time a woman's.

'No, my lord. The baby is yours.'

Mamillius ran from the room, down the corridor and one flight of stairs to the top of the great stairway, where he proceeded to shift himself carefully downwards on his bottom. At the bend in the stairway he stopped, peering over. The voices came from the great hall, where formal banquets were held.

At the threshold of the hall Paulina stood nursing a small bundle in her arms and his father stood before her, his face, in the glimmering light, still lividly pale.

Paulina took a step towards his father, who started backwards and put his arm up across his eyes.

'I have no wish to see the bastard. Or her mother the whore. Get away, witch, or by the gods I shall commit this whore's bastard to the flames and you along with it, hag.'

'Then it will be the torturer who is the heretic, not the burned. Look here at the child's face – your nose, your eyes, your lips, even your trick of frowning at the world. The gods know, the poor babe has reason enough to frown.'

'Polixenes' features.'

'A madman's words . . . my lord.' The title came as an exaggerated afterthought to the words that cut through the cold air. Mamillius gave an involuntary shudder. Were they going to fight? Paulina's thin form couldn't possibly worst his father's bulk.

But behind Paulina another presence appeared.

'Antigonus, rid us of your damnable shrew wife or by the gods I'll dispatch her for you.'

Paulina's husband took an uncertain step towards her, but Paulina, ignoring him, moved swiftly towards his father and laid the baby down before his feet. His father looked at her as if he might at any moment throw her to the ground beside it. Paulina stood rigid as a spear and very still in the candlelight. Then, as his father turned away, she too turned and walked past Mamillius, who had crept down the stairs and was crouching in the shadows of the stairwell. She came so close he smelt sweat. So Paulina was afraid.

Mamillius' heart was banging in his chest as, still barefoot, he followed Paulina down the long corridor that led to the courtyard. Crossing the wide space, he felt the freezing flags on his feet and the air bit his cheeks and tears smarted his eyes. He knew there were tears of emotion behind those conjured merely by the cold, but by concentrating hard he forced the sorrowful ones back. He moved stealthily towards the stables, and just beyond them, over a low wall, came Paulina's voice.

She was calling to Emilia, his old nurse, who had helped to bring him into the world and who would have been attending his mother as she gave birth for a second time.

'Emilia.'

'My lady?'

A smaller, dumpier presence joined the shadowy shape of Paulina.

'How is it with her?'

'Her body is weak, of course, but her heart and mind are strong. But the loss of her little girl . . .'

So his mother was alive, that was something. But not with her baby, and because he knew her, he knew how desperate that would make her feel.

'Will they let me see her?'

'No one but me can see her. Since you took the baby, my lady, you have been forbidden further entry.'

'And the boy?'

'Especially not the boy, on pain of death. Dear gods, madam, how will this end?'

'My husband has begged him to consult the oracle. We must pray that Apollo can bring enlightenment. You will take a message?'

'Anything. My poor lady.'

'Tell her the babe is with her father.'

'Oh, madam, was that wise?'

'It is best, Emilia.'

It is not best, Mamillius reflected. The look in his father's eyes had reminded him of a dog they once had that had gone mad. The dog had had to be drowned.

The two women stood murmuring but he ceased to try to listen. He was thinking hard. Should he try to see his mother or was it a better plan to try to find the baby and maybe rescue her? He preferred the former course but the latter would more likely be what his mother would want. Carefully, he moved back across the courtyard and re-entered the palace.

His father was in the great hall, still talking to Antigonus. Mamillius liked Antigonus. He was kind where Paulina was stern. Once, when he was still only six, Antigonus had given Mamillius a small bow and some arrows for him to shoot with, and the two of them had spent an enjoyable afternoon shooting crows. Paulina had scolded her husband and taken away the bow and arrows and Antigonus had winked at him behind her back and made a clacking motion with his hand. He was a good mimic and often made Mamillius laugh with his impersonations of various snooty courtiers; 'lickspittles', Antigonus called them. But there was nothing even faintly humorous about him now, standing before his father, holding a baby in his arms.

The baby began to yowl faintly and Antigonus began to rock stiffly back and forth on his heels.

'Take the bastard brat and burn it.'

'No, my lord. I cannot.'

Antigonus' voice, while still respectful, conveyed a note of firmness, which surprised Mamillius even as it heartened him.

'You disobey me?'

Mamillius waited for the answer but, perhaps wisely, the older man said nothing. Mamillius suddenly remembered how he had said nothing when Paulina had scolded him over the bow and arrows and saw for the first time that this was maybe a kind of strength.

In the scant light of the candlelit hall his father's face looked desperately ill. Mamillius had a sudden awful premonition that his father was about to die.

And then down the stairs there came a pattering and into the hall bounded Dash. His father visibly started. 'Back, sir, back to your room.'

Dash stood with his legs stiffened and simply stared

at his father. And then a very weird thing happened. The dog gave a great howl and the baby in Antigonus' arms began to yowl in turn.

Together, the hound and baby made the most melancholy chant that Mamillius had ever heard. It echoed down the great corridor as his father clapped his hands over his ears.

'Oh, gods, I am a feather blowing in the wind. Very well. Take the bastard as far from my dominions as you can and leave it as prey for kites and ravens. And be assured, if you deviate a whisker from this command in any respect, you, your wife and this wretched bastard child shall be put to a long torture before an assured death.'

And he turned and swept into the long darkness of the hall.

The hound stood stiff-legged, taut-backed, staring after him. Then his fine muzzle moved questingly. Mamillius uncurled himself out of the shadows, mutely putting out a hand to his dog, who nuzzled him cautiously.

Antigonus said not a word until the footsteps of the King had died away. Then he, in turn, put out a hand towards the boy, who moved into the protective curve of his arm.

'I'm sorry, my boy, that you should have had to witness that.'

Mamillius looked down at the stone flags and then, taking some obscure courage from this, up into the older man's face, grey in the half-light. 'Will you take her away?'

'Your sister, yes. I must.'

'And my – our mother?'

'Mamillius, I cannot afford to let her see your sister.'

'But why?' He was crying now and the baby began to cry faintly too, with a snuffling sound like the baby hedgepig he had found and fed last summer.

The older man bent down. 'Would you like to take her for a moment?' Clumsily, he rolled the little bundle into the boy's outstretched arms.

The baby looked up at Mamillius with wide blue eyes, eyes that were set off by a pair of eyebrows that made two quizzical dark semicircles, fine as if drawn by a pen. A candle guttered above and the child's eyes slid towards the flicker of light. Mamillius put out his forefinger and a tiny hand caught at it, clasping it tight.

'My sister,' the boy said. 'My little sister.'

A rush of tenderness overtook him. Never in all his born days had he felt such loving warmth for any creature. Not even his pet hedgepig, Snout, whom he had reared by hand, or the baby kestrel he had fed with grubs and beetles. Not even Dash when he was a half-bald pink puppy. This rosy little creature was his own blood.

'Where will you take her?'

'I don't know.' The man sighed and Mamillius felt his worried misery. 'I don't know. Somewhere far away. I must do as your father commands or . . .' He let the meaning trail away.

'You die?'

'As to that, I would prefer death to myself than to your sister. But I am afraid that if I do not do as your father orders then, then . . .'

'He might kill my mother?' Mamillius suggested. He could see now that that was possible. And then, a new prospect striking him, 'He might kill me?'

'I think not. But' – Antigonus' hand rested on the boy's shoulder – 'but it is true that your father is ill and not in his right mind. And when a man is not in his right mind, there's no knowing what ill patterns his mind may work in.'

'Let me come with you,' Mamillius said.

'No, my young madcap.'

'But why not?' Mamillius asked. 'I am forbidden to see my mother. My father is not himself. This – she – is my blood and my mother would want me to be with her.'

'Your mother would be worried sick and I –'

'You could say I stowed away,' said Mamillius with perfect logic. 'I could leave a note, if you like, to say I had run away until my parents made friends again. And then I could come with you. You could hide me until we're gone,' he said simply.

Antigonus reflected. It might be for the best. Impossible to say how the madness in Leontes might develop.

'Very well,' he said. 'I will speak to my wife and make

sure your mother knows what we are doing. You go and write your note and leave it where you can be sure no one finds it till we have left.'

Mamillius, who had sailed often round the coasts of Sicily, was unprepared for the swell of the open sea. But he loved the sense that there was nothing but water on all sides and no sight of land. Despite Antigonus' fears, no seasickness assailed him. Indeed, he made friends with the cabin boy, Matteo, who taught him to climb the mast to look out for dolphins and porpoises.

At night he slept in a cabin with his sister beside him in a little box bed, fashioned by the ship's carpenter, who had frankly fallen in love with the child. Indeed, so had most of the crew, who looked upon her not as any form of undesirable but a kind of lucky amulet, a changeling child, almost it seemed.

Mamillius had taken charge of his sister and Antigonus was patently relieved that he should do so. Having no children of his own, he found caring for a newborn baby, and a girl child at that, was not a skill that came naturally to him.

To Mamillius, however, it seemed to come as second nature. He cradled the little creature easily in his arms, brought up her wind and wiped her bottom with no disgust when she shat. The baby shit smelt, he announced, when a sailor with ten children asked if he would like the job taken off his hands, of no more than the watered goat's milk he fed her from the yield of Bella, the white-and-tan nanny goat which supplied the ship.

Mamillius often took his sister to see Bella, for some part of him felt the goat might offer some resonance of mothering to the baby, who had been so hideously parted from her own.

He missed his mother and spoke of her constantly. 'She loves you, little one. Don't fret, she may not seem to be here but she is with us. I dreamt of her again last night.'

The tilting ship and the interrupted nights, during which he tended the hungry baby, had lent a new quality to his dreams. Very often he dreamt of their mother – and always she was active, running, dancing, laughing, sometimes with his father too in the garden his father had had designed for her by a grand horticulturalist from Milan. A garden of roses and lilies, of sweet herbs and sparkling fountains. And a dovecot.

Mamillius told the baby about the white doves with the delicate coral feet which he fed on bread and milk.

Once he dreamt they were all flying in a strange device, like a bird but with wings of parchment. Mamillius thought: When I am older I will make such a machine. He thought often of Dash too and hoped the hound wasn't missing him too much. But he never dreamt of Dash.

Antigonus kept a certain distance from the pair. His parting from his wife had been painful, and not merely because he'd had to leave to undertake a task for which he had no stomach. Her rage against the King was so intense he feared she would use his son's departure in some vengeful way, and she had made it plain to him that were he to fulfil the King's command it would be the last he would see of her as a wife.

'Of course you must save the child,' she had insisted. 'Your life and mine are of no importance. That poor misguided fool will come to his senses and then what if you had followed orders whose footing stands in nothing more than insanity? You will be an accessory to murder – and very likely implicated in the death of the Queen, may the gods keep her blessed soul.'

Antigonus' sleep, like Mamillius', had been fitful but without the rewarding moth breath on his cheeks or the comfort of soft little limbs lying in his arms. Only the ravages of night sweats and cold anxieties.

Then there came a night of terrible storm and terrible sickness. Never a good sailor at best, Antigonus fell victim to the very disorder he had feared for his young companion. In the middle of the seemingly relentless torment he fell into a disturbing dream.

He woke, sick and exhausted, the following morning to a memory of the Queen's voice. 'You must leave my daughter in Bohemia.'

Bohemia was where the ship was already heading, since this was where Polixenes was King, and where he and Leontes' right-hand man, Camillo, had left for, once

Leontes' madness had made itself known. Antigonus had hoped for their counsel. But the apparition he had seen in his dream now troubled him. If the Queen wanted her child left in Bohemia, maybe the baby was Polixenes' child and not her husband's after all.

As he puzzled over this, there was a shout of 'Land ahead!' and hurrying up on deck he saw the misty outlines of Bohemia's coast. Mamillius, the baby as always in his arms, appeared up the cabin stairs and stood beside him.

'I dreamt of our mother last night,' he confided.

Antigonus stared down, torn between fear and pity. 'I too.'

'She told me my sister's name. Perdita, the lost one. It's a pretty name, don't you think?'

Antigonus looked down at the little face; the colour of her made him think of ripe apricots. 'Pretty enough.'

'I am going to take her to my Uncle Polixenes' court,' the boy continued. 'She'll be cared for there and he will know how I can send a message to our mother.'

'Maybe.'

'Why do you say "maybe"?'

'Mamillius, I –' but whatever he was about to say was interrupted by another glad cry of 'Land ahead!'

Mountains had lost their cloudy form and were clearly solid. Already a boat was being lowered, ready to take them ashore. Mamillius swung down a rope ladder and received his sister in his arms, handed down by the carpenter, who handed after her a wooden bird on a stick he'd carved from a piece of driftwood.

'Look, Perdita. A dove. Like the doves in our mother's cot at home.'

The bottom of the small boat rasped against pebbles and Mamillius, the baby in his arms, and Antigonus clambered out, leaving the sailor who had rowed them to pull back to the main ship.

'How shall we find our way to the palace?' Mamillius was eager now.

Antigonus put his hands to his head. He was lost. He was at a loss. He had no idea how he should proceed or what he should do with the children. He could not abandon the young prince; and it followed that he couldn't abandon the girl, bastard or not.

'Look,' he said. 'Let us find a place for you and the baby to rest while I get our bearings.'

'We shall need milk for Perdita soon,' Mamillius warned him.

In the room of justice in the palace the Queen stood. Denied a place to sit, she showed no sign of emotion other than the extremity of her pallor and the exacting straightness of her spine. She had been brought to hear the verdict of the oracle at Delphi. It had pronounced in her favour; yet still the mania gripped her husband.

'There is no truth in the oracle,' he had bellowed

and around the court fear had rippled. To denounce the oracle was a blasphemy.

But, as these impious words resounded in the shocked ears of the onlookers, the doors opened and a servant entered.

'What is the meaning of this interruption?'

'My lord, the Prince your son –'

'Yes?'

'Is gone.'

'Gone?'

The question hung in the still air. Behind the servant, the tall form of Paulina loomed. 'Dead, my lord.'

'Dead? How dead?'

'Dead of a broken heart.'

The Queen swayed and crumpled to the ground. And, long after, those who were present recalled the King's fearful cry. 'Apollo's angry and the heavens themselves strike at my injustice.'

The leather flask of Bella's milk was nearly gone and Perdita was asleep, snug beneath the fur of his bearskin coat. But she wouldn't sleep for much longer.

Mamillius looked yet again for any sign of Antigonus. He could no longer see the ship, which had been anchored in the bay, because the light was fading fast. It was growing colder and without the protection of his fur coat he shivered.

And then he heard a sound. Someone, up over the

hillock, was whistling. There was a pause and then a raucous voice began to sing.

Antigonus? Surely not. But at least it was a human being. Mamillius looked down at the sleeping Perdita, tucked the fur more closely round her and walked upwards in the direction of the singing voice. Reaching the top of the hillock he crouched behind a furze of juniper.

A man. A man dressed in bright-coloured ragged clothes and leading a bear. A scruffy man and an even scruffier bear. Mamillius, with his quick feeling for all creatures, felt his heart go out to the sad-looking animal.

The man stopped as if he had some kind of sixth sense and turned about. 'Hey there,' he called over towards Mamillius.

'Hello.' Mamillius, uncertainly, stepped out from the bush.

'Would you like to buy a ballad?' the man asked.

Mamillius was well brought up. 'I should be glad to,' he said. 'But I have no money with me at present.' The man began to turn away again, so, hastily, he added, 'But my father has money.'

The man turned back. 'Your father is –'

'Oh, he's King of Sicily,' Mamillius said. He waited for the man to be impressed.

'And I'm the King of China,' the man said. 'So long.'

'No, wait,' Mamillius said hurriedly. 'He really is the King, I promise. And the King of here is his friend.'

'Yeah?' said the man.

'Truly,' said Mamillius, desperate now. 'I, we, my friend and I were going to find him, the King here, I mean, but he's been gone a long time, my friend, and my sister's going to need food soon.'

At that moment a thin cry reached them from below.

'That's her,' Mamillius said. 'Please come with me. We need help.'

'Very well,' said the man. 'Tell you what. You stay here and mind the bear and I'll go and fetch your sister. I can't leave the bear and I don't want to drag it downhill. It's a sulky beast at best and it's in a mood today.'

'I could fetch her up,' Mamillius suggested, though he was tickled at the idea of looking after the bear.

'I'll get her,' said the man. 'Royal, you say. I suppose she's got something to show for it? Grand toys and so forth.'

'She's got a dove,' Mamillius said. 'It was made for her specially.'

'Ah,' said the man. 'Precious, I'll be bound.'

'Oh, yes,' Mamillius said. 'Very precious. She's right by the hawthorn brake at the bottom there.'

'Good,' said the man. 'I'll fetch her up here, then.'

Mamillius waited, holding the bear. He heard Perdita's cries abate. The man had obviously picked her up and it seemed that she was not afraid. He would help them to find the way to Uncle Polixenes and Uncle Polixenes would write to his mother and father and they would come to fetch him and Perdita home and all would be well again. Whatever had happened to make his father so angry must be over by now.

Minutes passed and the man didn't appear. The bear, which was sitting back on its haunches, as if relieved to be taking a rest, now lumbered to its feet and pulled at the leash. Uncertain what to do, Mamillius allowed himself to be led a few paces forwards. The bear moved its head ponderously on its great neck as if to check on this new constraint. Slowly it began to defecate. Partly out of a sense of tact and partly to escape the stench, Mamillius walked a little way down the slope of the hillock. A heather root tripped him and he fell, losing his grip on the rope.

Behind him he heard a great roar, and, turning sharply, he saw the bear lumbering away, its hindquarters still foul, towards a man coming from the opposite direction.

'Hey, there,' Mamillius called. 'Stop him. Stop the bear.'

To his intense horror he saw the bear rear up at the man, who cried terribly before his head was gripped by the great jaws. For a moment Mamillius stood frozen, not knowing what on earth to do. Then, putting his hands over his ears, he fled down the hillside towards where he had left the baby.

*

'He's not dead, my lady,' Paulina urged. 'He left a note. I found it in his bed. He went off with my husband and the baby.'

'But you said –'

'Your husband, forgive me, my lady' – Paulina did not look as if she felt herself in need of forgiveness – 'deserved a damn good scare. You saw how it brought him to his senses, madam,' she added, as an afterthought.

'But my poor husband.'

'Poor husband, my eye. My own husband had instructions to put your babe to death. But don't you fret. He's taken both children to Bohemia till the King comes to his senses. Let him stew in his own juice and you come with me awhile.'

Mamillius was sitting on the pebbled shore, crying. He cried harder, if less noisily, than the baby he had lost. He had watched a man die. Not merely die but being eaten alive. Antigonus, whom he had known all his life. Who had been only kind to him. Kind and brave. And he had lost his precious sister, his mother's newborn child. He had done terrible wrongs. He could never now go back to his mother.

Behind him the pebbles crunched.

'So you lost my bear?' It was the strange tattered man.

'I tripped,' Mamillius explained, still sobbing. 'I tripped and dropped the rope and he got away. And he ate my friend.'

'Well, he would. Ugly brute. The bear I'm talking about. I'm sorry about your friend but we're quits because I lost your baby.'

'Why did you?' Mamillius hit out wildly, too hurt, too heart-stricken, to care that his eight-year-old fist was no match for this hard-handed man of the road.

'Now then, steady on. Someone got to the infant first. I saw an old boy carry her off and then I heard the bear carrying on so I came back to try to catch him. No good. He'd scarpered. He'll have had a taste of living flesh now and once they've had that there's no managing them again. He'll be off after someone's sheep or worse. Be thankful he didn't get your babe. I'd say it's the gods doing, her being taken like that. She'll be fine. Take my word for it.'

'You saw where my sister went?'

'No. I saw her being taken, that's all.'

'Can we go after her?'

'You know what?' said the man. 'I think best I take you back to that ship I saw anchored out there in the bay. If you're who you say you are, there'll be a prize for returning you.'

'Oh, no,' Mamillius said. 'I can't go back. Not yet. I must find my sister.'

'I reckon we'll do that better with help,' the man said. 'Reinforcements. See?'

*

Alone in his private chamber the King sat, as he always did these days, drowned in dark despair. No wife. No child. No friends. Only his boy's hound to keep him company, and even the dog appeared merely to suffer his presence. The dog was pining, as he was, for the lost boy. But at least the creature was some bulwark against that terrible daily scourge to his conscience, Paulina. She had grown even more scathing now that it seemed her husband had died, along with his daughter. What further ill could life throw at him?

A servant entered, bowing low. These days, the servants were wary of him, not knowing when another bout of madness might strike. He had had his daughter put to death, thereby killing his beloved son and his wife, who was always, in the servants' view, by far the more approachable of the royal couple. 'My lord.' This was going to be tricky.

'Yes?'

'My lord, there is a man, a man come.'

'Yes?'

'He says, my lord, he says he has brought back your son.'

The King rose from his seat.

'Scoundrel,' he bellowed. 'Monster. Villain. Abomination. I have no son. My son is dead. Dead, dead, dead. Tell this piece of crooked vileness to go and never come near this palace again or I swear I will have him strung up and his corpse thrown to the wolves.'

'Well,' the tattered man said to the boy, 'I am sorry to tell you this, but it's best you know that your mother is dead and your father doesn't want you. Since you've lost me my bear, you'd better come along with me. I'll teach you tricks. We'll scratch out a living.'

The boy nodded. The ship in which he had sailed to Bohemia had vanished, and it had been a long, wearisome trek back to Sicily. Grief had worked a deep change in him and he had grown, on the journey, finally mute.

'I can't say as it's an easy life,' the tattered man went on. 'But I was talking to the fellow who was told to send me packing and from what I heard from him about your court life it was pretty dismal. Dangerous too. The life of a vagabond isn't beer and skittles, but it isn't all hard graft either, and at least there's some jollity along the way. Are you game?'

Mamillius nodded.

'That's as well, as I wouldn't say you had much choice. But, see, spring's around the corner,' the tattered man said. 'I smell it in the air. And then there's summer and harvest festivals and sheep-shearing and ballad-selling and fairs. You can call me Autolycus, by the way. It's one of my names. We'll have a grand time together, you and me. You'll see.'

At twenty-four, Mamillius had long parted from Autolycus. He had learnt to be an accomplished juggler, fortune-teller, card-sharper and occasional pickpocket.

But his true gift proved to be in storytelling. On days when ballad-sheets were in short supply he had composed brand-new ones for his master, who, having an eye for a good commercial enterprise, had set him to write stories to sell to those who could read and to perform for those who could not. One evening, they fell into company with a troupe of travelling players who, on hearing of the boy's gifts, which Autolycus was boasting of, invited this piece of proven talent to join them. Autolycus had raised objections but the actor-manager was a forceful man and Autolycus, who was at heart a loner, soon abandoned his objections – which, based on principle rather than desire, were flimsy anyway – and, quite civilly, let his young apprentice go.

Since then, Mamillius, now known as 'Mouse' (a corruption of 'Muse', which was the teasing nickname awarded him by one of the admiring company), had become a writer of renown. The plays he wrote attracted audiences wherever they travelled and he had come to relish the life: the camaraderie of colleagues, the excitement of shows and appreciative audiences, the deeper thrill of writing the plays, conjuring words from the recesses of his unknown mind as once he had conjured doves out of handkerchiefs.

Now they had come to Sicily, where it seemed some great event was occurring. He was in the inn, enjoying a pot of local wine, when Flavio, their manager, came in.

'Mouse, get your best quill out and sharpen it. We're summoned to put on one of your blessed plays at court.'

'Why so?'

'Seems there's some big celebration afoot. The lost daughter of the King's returned and his wife's back from the grave. Hey, what's up, Mouse?' For his colleague, closing his eyes, had turned whey pale.

'It was like a blush in reverse, if you get my meaning,' Flavio said later, when he was describing this to another member of the company. 'As if snow had entered his veins. I didn't hardly recognize him.'

As this conversation was taking place, Mouse was walking feverishly about the town. Everywhere was abuzz with the news. Perdita, their lost Princess, had arrived with the Crown Prince of Bohemia, whom she was to marry; and, more miraculous still, her mother, also supposed dead, had reappeared. No one, he couldn't help observing, spoke of the one member of the royal household who had not come back from the dead. Did his mother ever wonder if he might be alive? But maybe when the news came that Antigonus had perished on his unholy mission, the boy he had taken with him was also believed lost for all time.

All night he walked through the town. He had been a stranger to that life for so long – sixteen years, it must be, during which everything he'd been born to had been lost – that when Flavio suggested Sicily as their next port of call, really on a whim, as sometimes took him,

Mouse almost failed to register its significance. The life of a playwright had so engaged him that the life of a young prince at court had dwindled in his mind to nothing more substantial than a dream. Nightmare, more truly, he thought, passing through an alley where he had once gone with his mother to visit a sick subject for whom his mother had conceived a characteristic concern: the dreadful doings that night in the palace, the devoured Antigonus, his lost baby sister.

Could he bear it, he pondered, noting in passing the unintended word play that his perpetually riddling mind couldn't resist throwing in. And did he anyway want to be drawn back into that life? He had the life he'd made for himself, a life that, for all its perilousness, had its own riches, which would be incompatible with a return to that other, more material wealth that must accompany royal status.

But then, to see his mother again. And his baby sister, grown to graceful womanhood. For all the likely exaggeration, the word on the street was that she was unusually lovely.

Well, he would write them a play and it would be such a play as he'd never written before and he would, as always, perform one of the minor roles. That way he would at least have sight of his lost family.

The palace Master of Ceremonies had compressed his rather withered lips when told that he could have no information about the play in advance of its performance. Luckily for the company Mouse's reputation had earned him the right to artistic silence and not even Flavio was given any hint of what their playwright was brewing up for them. Flavio grumbled about the props and accessories that were, somewhat magisterially, requested of him. 'A bear? Where for crying out loud are we going to get a bear at this short notice?' But now the play was written, rehearsed, the bear, whose teeth had been removed by its owner, had settled quite docilely into its part and they were all prepared. The palace room where they were to perform had been cleared, and the very select audience that had been invited was seated and waiting expectantly.

Mouse had allocated himself the introduction of the play, which was to be followed by a prologue delivered by Time, whose role was to lead their imaginations back down the vista of years to a man sitting in a graveyard. He had never followed up that man, whose story had been broken off so violently all those years ago. Time for that long-lost soul to recover his voice.

'You're on, Mouse,' the prompt murmured. 'Break a leg.'

The man who had been born a prince walked forward into the marble-floored courtroom where once he had played at marbles. From the light of the candle-sconces which graced the walls he could see the faces of the audience, especially those of the six figures ranged along the front row: his mother, father, sister and her prince, Uncle Polixenes and Aunt Paulina.

'Your royal highnesses,' he began, and his voice came hesitatingly and cracked, so for a horrible moment he feared he was going to cry. 'Lords, ladies and gentlemen,' he said, his voice gathering strength. 'We present you with *The Midsummer's Tale*, for' – he bowed low, sweeping from his head the velvet Venetian hat he had chosen for this appearance – 'a merry tale is best for summer.'

It was generally agreed that the play was a terrific success. The royal audience had laughed, wept, cheered and clapped enthusiastically as the players took them from the graveyard, haunted by sprites and goblins, revenants and fairies, to a rural sojourn of shepherds and shepherdesses, where a tyrannical king abandoned his throne and took up the life of a contemplative. The bear, most especially, was a hit and had been received with rapturous applause.

The royal family had been pressing in their request to meet the author at the play's conclusion, but from the moment he left the stage, where he had been playing a minor role as one of the rural clowns, the successful author had been nowhere to be found. No one noticed that young master Tobias, who had played the boy in the churchyard so convincingly, had also vanished from the party. He was, as it happened, with the author, who, palpably drunk, was walking, his arm across Tobias's shoulder, by the seashore.

'You see, Toby,' the playwright said, stopping to trace a bare foot in the damp sand, 'you can't go back. That's the devil of it, if it isn't a blessing, which you know, it may be. You make your life, or, rather, I should say, life makes you, but there's no returns. No returns,' he said again, offering the bottle to his young friend.

He had observed his mother, little different from the majestic comely woman in his mind, only older, more lined; he had seen his sister, who, if not quite as wondrously beautiful as the rumours had made out, was certainly a fresh-complexioned, pretty young girl; and he had seen his father, his firm upright carriage bent into a sorry stoop, his once-black brows wild and white, and his broad proud face sunken-cheeked – and the sight of this last is what had undone him.

He couldn't go back. He had maybe saved his sister – he would like now to think so – and she must carry the aftermath of all they had been through. He had played his part. And if he was still a small, unresolved tenderness in their hearts, that would have to do.

'Come, young Toby,' he said flinging an arm across the shoulders of the boy beside him, who was now skimming stones across the moon-spangled surface of the darkly receding sea. 'Let us walk and talk and drink the night away, for autumn is in the air, I can smell it, and we mortals are written on sand and there's only so much time left to us to play.'

The Sofa

———◄○►———

When my mother died, I decided to move into the Hampstead flat that had belonged to my parents. My wife, Jennifer, and I were divorcing and I was concerned about where I should live. To move into my old family flat would save me the expense of renting, or another mortgage; and it would offer my children a familiar place to come and stay.

My father had died some years earlier and my mother had lingered on in the flat, more and more resembling some pale moth fluttering frailly across the soft-carpeted floors of the dimly lighted rooms. Towards the end, she rambled a bit about her childhood, which had been a hard one, so it was no surprise it was still on her mind. Once she mistook me for her brother Max, who was long gone by this time.

My parents, to my mind, had been an archetypal couple: my father, an amiably aggressive, enterprising man, had made his name, and a modest fortune, as a solicitor dealing in company law. The precise details of his work bored me; and it hurts me to confess that I have as misty a notion now of quite what it was that he did as I had as a callow young man. Whatever it was, it ensured for my brother and me what used to be called 'a good education', comfortable holidays abroad and sufficient spare funds to allow our father to look rueful when we overdrew our bank accounts but always to come up with the means to make good the deficits. My mother served whatever needs my father had to make this enterprise run smoothly. She fed him, listened attentively to the daily details of his working life, absorbed his tempers and nursed him faithfully in his last years when he became demented.

Over the dementia I fear I was a broken reed. My elder brother, Simon, as always, put me to shame. He visited our parents dutifully, read to my father from his beloved Conan Doyle and Swinburne, and allowed my mother to shed occasional tears without the swift instinctive aversion with which I always met such displays.

But then, I was my mother's child, the favoured younger son. Parents are not supposed to have favourites, but, as all children know, they do. 'Ah,' my mother would sigh, when she believed I was out of earshot, 'Simon has his father's brains, but Nathan is the *sensitive* one. He takes after my side of the family.'

My mother's 'side of the family' were refugees from Belgium. They had escaped Hitler at the eleventh hour with a few portable heirlooms and a bag of uncut diamonds, rescued from the premises of my grandfather's diamond-cutting business. The diamonds had been entrusted to my mother's younger brother, Max. It was considered that a tow-headed five-year-old would be the least likely target for a Gestapo spot check, and the prize specimens of my grandfather's business were sewn into the lining of Max's trousers.

Somewhere along the fraught journey to safety, the bag sprang a leak; so that by the time the family reached England – chastened, at their changed fortunes, yet jubilant at their successfully negotiated escape – only one lump of diamond rock was found to have survived. My uncle-to-be had seemingly been leaking diamonds as the family made their way across occupied France – first in the Daimler, donated by a valued Antwerp customer, and then on the rickety boat that, with his last handful of hard currency, my grandfather had bought in order to cross the Channel to freedom.

My uncle never got over this calamity. Aside from his immediate family he was incapable of relationships, remaining single until he died, a prisoner of tyrannical and implacable obsessions. Relentless hand-washing, incessant closing and re-closing of doors, checking and rechecking of locked windows, counting the precise number of footsteps it took him to walk down the hall was too full time an activity to allow space for another person's ordinary anxiety. The pale lanky relic of that small scared boy could never again risk failing another's trust.

But as a boy myself I was fond of my uncle. My brother

and I would be sent to visit him in his house in Finchley. We played, rather inhibitedly, in his garden, knocking conkers from the horse chestnut tree, and sometimes Uncle Max would play the piano for us, Schubert and Chopin and Schumann and just occasionally, when he was in one of his rare moods of mirthfulness, jazz.

We sat on his stoutly upholstered yellow Chesterfield while he played and I used to push small items down the back of it, checking to see if they were still there on any following visit. They always were; Uncle Max, for all his obsessionalism, was not house proud.

After the war, my grandfather started a successful importing business. There was no need to cash in the sole survivor of the family's earlier fortunes, and the diamond was cut, by my grandfather, into a magnificent many-faceted brilliant, which was splendidly displayed on my grandmother's strong red hand till the day she died. It was willed to my mother. Unlike my grandmother, my mother wore the diamond only on special occasions. Indeed, as a child I came to recognize 'an occasion' by the diamond's reappearance. I would watch it glinting in its cleansing soak: a glass of gin, to 'bring up the shine', as my mother said. She tipped the gin down the sink afterwards with some reluctance. 'Seems a shame,' she would say, 'but I couldn't risk your father catching something from it.' She herself drank nothing stronger than sherry.

Then, one day, the diamond disappeared. My mother went frantic with worry. She had worn it, she remembered – how could she forget? – at Uncle Max's funeral. Several female relatives, reconvened from far-flung distances for the event, had enthused over the ring and my mother had reminded them of the story. 'Poor Maxie,' she had said, wiping her eyes. 'How he sobbed when we discovered the diamonds had gone. He never got over it, you know? He didn't even like to see me wear this one.' Thoughtfully, she twisted the ring round her slight finger. Unlike her own mother, my mother had the smallest hands. But after Maxie's funeral, she told us, plaiting her fingers in consternation, she had put the ring away – she *knew* she had – as she always did, in the green leather velour-lined box, where she kept her few bits of jewellery. She would have known for sure if it were missing at the time.

For a good while, the missing ring was a conundrum. Our cleaner, Mrs Bevis, the window cleaner, Steve, passing tradesmen, even family friends were anxiously considered as likely candidates for jewel robbers. But my mother's history had prejudiced her in favour of a benign universe, and even with evidence of wrongdoing she disliked harbouring 'uncharitable thoughts'. In the end, she persuaded herself that a magpie had taken the ring – the time she took the box out to look for her pink pearls and got interrupted by the Kleen-Eezy man. The story didn't convince the rest of us, but it seemed kinder to let her continue with this far-fetched explanation unmolested.

When Uncle Max's will was read, it turned out he had

left his money, quite a tidy sum, to a Jewish pro-Palestinian charity. There were very few 'effects'. The piano was to go to my brother, I had an unremarkable picture of some cows drinking, and my mother was left the yellow velvet Chesterfield, by this time very shabby and much in need of repair. My mother was not best pleased about the money. Not that she ever wanted it for herself. 'You could have done with some of that money,' she said to me, when she had finally accepted that Jennifer and I were going to divorce. 'You're not going to give her the house as well, are you?'

The cost of having my uncle's legacy restored proved to be over two thousand pounds. My father, ever pragmatic, wanted to chuck the sofa out; but family sentiment reigned supreme in my mother. 'I can't,' she said. 'It wouldn't be right. Poor Maxie. He never got right after losing those diamonds. I'll cover it with a throw and some nice cushions. You won't be able to see the holes.'

It was an irony, then, that in my father's last years it was the Chesterfield he took to lying on, his once sturdy limbs covered by his dressing gown, mumbling, or starting at inaudible voices. My mother would sit with him, her small hand in his big, freckled one, never seeming to resent that the man who had protected her all her adult life had become a helpless baby. On one of my too rare visits she told me: 'You know, Natty, I fell asleep holding Arthur's hand and I woke in the night, not knowing where I was and I thought it was Max lying there.'

'Well, it is Max's sofa,' I said.

'I suppose that's it. Funny thing, he was crying and saying sorry – it was as if he were a little boy again and had lost those diamonds. He never got over those diamonds.'

When I moved into the flat I put off dealing with my parents' things for several months. The process of divorce, and the move itself, had taken it out of me. And I knew I was going to have to steel myself to dispose of my mother's accumulated pickings. In the end, I schooled myself to do it room by room: mountains of china were carted to charity shops, one or two plates fetched a dispiritingly small sum at auction; books were sent to hospitals; my brother's children bagged the best of the furniture; and I gave Jennifer the one painting of value that my mother had bought. It was a good idea, for it took some of the sting out of what we had been through and I never cared for it myself. She came over to fetch it and we stood in the sitting room, where we had often stood together in the days when we felt we might make things work between us.

'What are you going to do with this?' she inquired, gesturing at the sofa. It was not only worn by now, it looked sinisterly stained.

'I don't know,' I admitted. 'I'd really like to chuck it out but –'

'But sentiment forbids?' Jennifer laughed, though not unkindly. My mother's attachment to her family had been a sore point between us.

'I'll think about it,' I said, a little stiffly. I felt that at least I no longer had any need to justify my own sentiments to Jennifer.

Two days later I met Ella Wheelwright in Sainsbury's. I'd not seen her for twenty years, not since we'd been at university together, but in all those years there was probably not a month when I hadn't thought about her. She looked much the same. Unusually upright, and with fine fair hair and freckles.

'Hello, darling,' she said, as if we had parted that morning. 'I saw you shopping here the other day and yelled, but you ignored me.'

'I would never ignore you, Ella,' I said.

'Well, darling,' she said. 'Here we are in Sainsbury's. What would you like to do?'

I asked her back to the flat for coffee, and really only to say something – because I was at a loss where to start after all this time – I showed her the sofa, describing its history. 'I think I'll have to throw it out,' I said.

'Oh, you mustn't.'

'Why not?' I rather hoped she would rescue it from me and relieve me from the responsibility. Ella Wheelwright was like that.

'It's your history,' she said. 'You can't throw out your history. Even that.' She was looking at one of my father's more intimate stains.

'I know,' I said. 'You're right.' That was the thing about Ella Wheelwright. She tended to be right.

I was as good as my word – or the word I'd tacitly given to Ella – and two weeks later I cleared the room so that the gloomy-sounding Irish upholsterer, whom Ella had found for me, could take the sofa off in his van. Waiting for the sofa's redeemers I sat on it, and tried to recall Uncle Max playing Schubert. And then I remembered the plastic khaki-coloured soldier it had been my habit to post down the sofa's sides. I reposted him every visit we made, and I had no recollection of ever having recovered my toy from its hiding place. It seemed unlikely he had survived so long undiscovered, but nonetheless I pushed exploring fingers down. The inevitable old biro, paper clips, a rubber band and, yes, something small and light. I pulled it out, along with a good deal of fluff, and looked at it in my hand. Winking in the sun, which was striking the window, was my mother's diamond.

And when Ella rang me a few days later I sort of knew what she was going to say. Even for her, she sounded excited. 'Darling, listen. You won't believe this, but Mick has just found a bag of stones in the innards of your uncle's sofa. He thinks they're uncut diamonds.'

A Christmas Gift

---◀〇▶---

'I hate Christmas.'

The words sounded starker to her own ears than Frances Travers had quite intended but once out she could hardly take them back. In any case, she was talking to her old friend, Prue, who was practised at ignoring her excesses.

'You didn't used to hate it. I remember you decorating the tree in Steeple Aston and us laughing fit to bust at Alan's dreadful choice of knickers for me.'

Prue and Frances had been friends since the days when their husbands had shared lifts to work in Oxford from the rural village where both, with young families at that time, lived. Frances and Prue had likewise shared the transport of their children. Children are perhaps a more lasting cement for friendship than a daily journey to work.

'That was then. It's not the same now.'

It wasn't in so many ways. Aside from the march of time, which had inevitably changed them both, Prue's husband Alan had absconded with the man who was contracted to clean their office windows and Frances's husband, Dan, had died suddenly from a galloping cancer.

'Not the same in general or for you in particular?' Frances had sometimes wondered if Prue's husband's flight with the window cleaner was in part an escape from his wife's obsession with precision.

'Oh, I don't know,' she said now, regretting that she had raised the topic. But Prue had rung just as she had put down the phone to her daughter, Anna.

Her son, Jacob, had been less insistent than his sister in his invitation but that was in his character. The point was both had asked her for Christmas and she knew in her bones that, while neither really wanted her, if she went to either there would be trouble.

Since Dan's death she was always in trouble, one way or another, with her children. Among her many reasons for missing her husband was a shocked and growing awareness that even one's children attack the vulnerable. Maybe, she reflected, especially one's children. Maybe it's some obscure aspect of evolutionary survival.

It had never occurred to her to be afraid of being a solitary woman. She and Dan had enjoyed a shared independence, neither demanding total attention from the other; relishing each other's company, with the inevitable ups and downs, when they were together. She knew when he died how badly she would miss him. What she had not calculated was that his presence had provided a certain safety. Although she didn't like admitting it nowadays, she often felt bullied. Bullied and, this was harder to acknowledge, faintly despised.

'I'd ask you to mine,' Prue said, 'but my mother's coming and –'

'No, no, it's fine,' Frances interrupted. 'I'll think of something.'

'Why not say you've been invited somewhere else?'

'Where? They know all my friends. They'd ring me there, or Anna would anyway, and find I wasn't.'

'Oh, I don't know,' Prue said, becoming bored of the subject. 'Tell them you have a secret lover or something.'

Although Frances had taken this last suggestion as one of Prue's flippancies, the idea strangely took hold. Why shouldn't she have a secret lover? She was only fifty-five and looked, she'd been told, ten years younger. Men, she had been assured, still found her attractive. That she had not found any man she had met since Dan's death sufficiently attractive to settle with was neither here nor there. A fictional lover could be constructed. It might also, she began to think, encourage a change of attitude in her children.

She spent some time envisaging this phantom paramour. For a while she toyed with the image of a younger man, but she was a woman of good sense and reason told her a younger man would breed in her insecurity. No, the new lover would be in his sixties. Grey haired, but once dark (as she had once said to Prue, men had to be dark), well dressed, but not over concerned with fashion. Quite possibly he was French, or Italian, or even, throwing fancy further to the winds, Australian. The one time she had contemplated infidelity to Dan it was with an Australian. It had left her with the view – probably a prejudice, she thought – that Australian men were more direct than the English. And braver. Any new consort, she decided, must be brave.

She spent an enjoyable time considering the question of her lover's profession. An architect? That would work well with her own profession of industrial designer. A politician was out because that would entail a public life too easy to disprove. But he would need to hold strong political views. Left-wing ones, certainly. She settled finally on an art historian, with a university background. That gave them shared tastes and would allow scope for travel.

His marital status was easier. He couldn't be a bachelor, as that would give rise to questions from Anna about his sexuality. It might be best if he was a widower to match her widowhood. Or at least long-since divorced.

By the time her daughter rang again Frances's lover was promisingly fleshed out. He was half Scottish (on his father's side), half Italian, a former professor in Milan (not as traceable as, say, Glasgow or Edinburgh), and she had met him at an exhibition at the Courtauld. She had foolishly left her umbrella at the café table where he was also taking coffee and he, noticing the omission, had courteously come after her with it. It was that unusual jade-green umbrella she'd bought in Paris. They had found they were headed for the same bus stop, and the same bus, the number 9, and one thing had led to another.

'But, Mum, you've never mentioned him.'

'Well, darling, I wasn't sure, you know, that it was serious and I don't necessarily tell you everything about my life.'

There was a pause at the other end of the phone and, safely obscured by distance, Frances smiled.

'But who is he? Is he safe?'

So like her daughter, who, for all her mother's competence as a driver, still refused to allow her to transport her children. 'Oh, very safe.' This was going to be good fun. 'He's an art historian. He'd been at the Courtauld to advise on a drawing.'

'And is he married?' Anna's voice conveyed a tincture of reproval.

'Of course not, darling. I'm not a man snatcher.' A slight hint of offence in her own tone seemed appropriate. 'He's divorced.'

'You should be careful with divorced men. He might just be using you.'

'The decree was seventeen years ago. I imagine he's got over it.'

'Does he have children?'

Stupid of her. She'd not worked out his position on children. Swiftly, hoping there was no perceptible pause to betray any indecision, she offered up 'A son and a daughter, but they're both long grown up.'

'Like you, then?'

'I suppose,' Frances said, wondering if it was a strain of jealousy in Anna's voice that she was detecting. 'I've not met them,' she added, not wishing to hurt her daughter by displaying too much interest in her lover's offspring.

'Well,' Anna said. 'I suppose he could come here too. What's he called, by the way?'

'That's sweet of you, darling, but we thought we might go away.' She hadn't quite settled on a name for her new companion and was hoping for more time. Names are important.

Luckily, Anna decided that she had to go, only adding that she hoped Jacob wouldn't be worried at this news.

Jacob, however, was relieved, she guessed, to have the prospect of his mother off his hands. He asked fewer questions than his elder sibling, only inquiring where she planned to go.

And 'Venice' was her surprising answer, surprising only because she had hitherto had thoughts of somewhere like the Lake District.

'Will you be okay with that?'

She knew why he was asking. It was the last holiday she'd taken with Dan. It was there that the first mortal symptoms had declared themselves and they had flown home early to a doctor to receive the dread news.

But the destination with her new lover had been spoken unconsciously, so she assumed it must be right.

'Perfectly. It's time to go back.'

'Well, good luck with it, Mum. We'll see you before you go?'

Neither of her children had pressed Frances about her lover's name, which was as well, she reflected, as she waited at the quayside at Marco Polo Airport for the boat to take her to San Stae. She herself had still not settled on a name. But it would come to her, she felt sure, as she passed these intimate days with him. She would get to know him better as they walked together, visited churches, and galleries, shopped, ate and made love. She had to mentally shake herself a little when she realized she was looking forward to the last.

She had decided an apartment would suit her better than a hotel. She could cook there and lounge about in more freedom. And she and whatever his name was needed a degree of space. An apartment was less likely to have an en suite bathroom with thin walls, which might lead to embarrassment in the early days of intimacy.

And it was a good choice, she reflected, as the young bearded Italian showed her round. The apartment was spacious, with two bathrooms – a blessing for any relationship, however familiar – and two bedrooms hung with heavy Venetian fabrics, and over-welcoming, capacious beds. The young man advised about the heating system, the bewildering complexities of the rubbish disposal, warned her about a sticking shutter and then regretted, in perfect English, that he 'must dash'.

The Campo San Giacomo dell'Orio is one of Venice's most domestic areas, where children out of school still play hopscotch and blithely shoot footballs against the goal of the billowing walls of the charming thirteenth-century church. On bright winter days old men, splendid in copious and colourful scarfs, lounge in the sun reading their newspapers while mothers sit by them and chat, rocking their equally well-muffled babies. And the gods were being kind to her, for it was just such a brilliant golden day as she strolled through the campo taking the measure of her environment.

There was a supermarket, a baker's exuding delicious smells of vanilla – and why, for heaven's sake, was that never possible in England? – and, by a bridge in a nearby calle, a wine shop which, for two euros, decanted wine from barrels into plastic bottles (one euro extra for the bottle). What more could she ask?

She would buy litres of wine from the Veneto and eat exactly what she felt like: artichokes, large tomatoes, little frizzy greens, salty provolone cheese, walnut bread, chestnuts, dense black grapes and leafy clustered clementines. There would be no question of turkey.

Deciding to inspect the church, she was startled to be commanded to pay. '*Per pregare?*' she inquired and was grudgingly admitted without having to cough up the tourist tariff. Well, but she did want to pray. She wanted to give thanks for the excellent outcome of her lucky inspiration. If there was a God, he deserved her thanks.

A Byzantine cross painted with a mournful twisted Christ hung suspended in the dim air before the altar and dutiful to her implied promise she sat head bowed awhile before getting up to examine the altarpiece behind. A badly lit notice informed her it was the Virgin with Saints by Lorenzo Lotto (*c.* MDXLVI).

'The only Lotto altar left in Venice,' a voice behind her said.

A man. A man with greying hair, possibly in his sixties.

'Yes?'

'Sadly, because he is, I think, one of the best artists Venice produced. You know this church?'

'Not really. I've just arrived. But I like it.'

'It may be the oldest in Venice. Its foundations are ninth century.'

'I'm afraid I've read nothing about it yet.'

'It's certainly to my mind one of the most agreeable. Come and see the column that Ruskin admired.'

He took her to inspect a dark green marble column topped with the curling ram's horn ionic capital.

'I like Ruskin,' she said. She seemed to have lost her usually rich vocabulary.

'Yes. He knew his own mind.'

'That's good.' She must sound like an idiot.

'Essential to know one's mind, I believe.'

'Oh, yes.'

'I have spent years getting to know my own. You are staying near here?'

'In an apartment just around the corner.'

'Me too. I'm visiting my daughter, who had the good sense to marry a Venetian and the even better sense to live in this sestiere. My son, on the other hand, has married an American who lives in Kansas but you can't win 'em all. May I give you coffee? The place in the campo is pricey but you do get the sun.'

'He's called Alec,' Frances told her daughter the following week when she rang to inquire about the holiday. 'His daughter lives in Venice so he knows it well. And of course he's an art historian so –'

'That's great. As long as you're sure, Mum.'

'Well, I wasn't,' Frances said gravely. 'These things take time to develop. But –'

'Spending a holiday together,' Anna agreed. 'It does sort of –'

'Absolutely,' Frances interrupted, wishing to deflect any trespass on her wholly delightful escapade and shelving the moment when the companion she had spent those delightful days with might have to disappear. 'It gives a kind of substance to one's vague fantasizing.'

Vacation

'What the *hell* does she want from you?' Beth asked for the third time. Hamish was negotiating the car on to the M1. The start of their holiday had been delayed by the lateness of the hour at which they had finally got to bed. Never mind sleep.

'Darling,' Hamish's mother had written. 'Stefan died suddenly last Thursday. We cremated him today. May I throw myself on your mercy and come? Blessings, Una.'

'Why now?' Beth had asked. 'For Christ's sake, why must she come now? And why "Blessings"? She's not remotely religious.'

'Because she's my mother. Because I'm her only son and there's no one else. Because I can't just say, "Sorry, Ma, we're on holiday" when there's room for her to come too.'

'Hardly "room". Two bedrooms and I'll bet they're tiny. And you never call her "Ma".'

'That's not what you said when we rented it!' Women, Hamish thought, always redefined experience to fit their argument.

'Why not say, "Sorry, we're on holiday"? She sent *you* away when it suited her. She didn't give a damn about Stefan – only his obscene bank balance. She didn't even ask you to the funeral. It was a marriage of convenience for her. You've always said so.'

Hamish's father had died of leukaemia when his only child was eighteen months. Barely a year later, his widow remarried a Swiss banker thirty years her senior. When Hamish was not quite five he was sent back to England as a boarder at Stefan's old prep school. Thereafter, the banker stumped up any finance needed to keep his wife's only child well dressed, well educated and at a distance.

'Because I can't.'

The Sancerre he had brought home because it was Beth's favourite was finished and she had resorted to a bottle of cheap Spanish red. She had started to drink more, Hamish noted.

'I don't think I'll come.' Beth spoke with the careful diction of the not-yet-quite drunk. 'You go. Take "Ma" with you with my *blessings*. I'll stay here.'

'Bethy!'

'I loathe it when you call me that when we're having a row.'

While Beth was in the bath, Hamish rang his mother in

Zurich. Beth heard him say, 'I'll pick you up at Glasgow Airport,' and then something she couldn't catch.

'What did you tell her?' She was out of the bath and towelling herself dry. She was a handsome woman, Hamish thought, yet he felt no desire for her. He wished he did. In his heart of hearts (Wherever *that* is! Beth would say) he didn't like his assistant Nicky, the girl he seemed to be having an affair with. But Nicky had what Beth had never had: the ability to make him feel he was lucky to be with her. Beth was stoical and faithful. Fidelity, for reasons hard to account for, is rarely sexually attractive.

'I told her that she could stay the first few days with us and then I would find her a hotel.'

'There *is* no hotel on the island.'

'We can ship her over to the mainland. Come on, Bethy, what's done cannot be undone.'

'That's *Macbeth*,' Beth said. 'Not exactly a comforting reference. And don't call me that.' She pulled on her pyjamas and climbed into bed. Turning her back to him, she said, 'It's not true, anyway, about *Macbeth*. It's never too late. That's the point. It's called irony.'

Near Doncaster, she brought up the subject of his mother again.

'How can she do this? Ignore you for thirty-odd years and just pick you up when it suits her. It's a fucking cheek.'

'I dislike the fashion of saying "fuck" at every turn,'

Beth had recently opined at a dinner party. 'I prefer to use the word accurately.'

Hamish rejected the notion of reminding her of this. Watching, in his rear mirror, a juggernaut lumbering alongside them in the next lane, he was assailed by a desire to pull over into its path and be smashed to smithereens. 'I wouldn't say she ignored me, exactly.'

'What would you say, then?'

'Beth, I'm driving. I don't want to have an accident talking about my mother.'

'There you are,' Beth said. 'That says it all.'

South-west of Oban, they crossed an elderly grey stone bridge, which, since the eighteenth century, has connected the mainland to Seil, one of the Slate Islands off the west coast of Argyll. They were met at the island's northerly point by Andy, who was to ferry them across to the tiny island off Seil's northern tip.

Andy's navy wool hat was jammed over a flat freckled face, which bore, Hamish detected, an expression of impertinent resentment. His hair was the orange of a ginger tom. Under Andy's direction, Hamish backed the car into a dangerously narrow space, hitting a bollard and badly pitting the back bumper.

Andy began to sling their luggage into the motorboat, which was littered with damp cigarette packets, silver paper and Mars-bar wrappers. A pair of old binoculars lay on one of the seats. He handed down his passengers carelessly, started up the motor and they sheered violently off, knocking Hamish sideways.

'Oh, Hamish, look, seals.'

'Where?'

'Over there, by those rocks.'

'Be seals, all right,' said Andy, nodding as if he owned them. 'Here.' He handed Beth the binoculars. His pale, red-rimmed eyes creased cannily as if he had already reckoned up her husband's failings and was offering himself as an ally.

The smooth round heads of the seals looked avuncular. Beth pictured herself swimming beside their sleek bodies with the cold Atlantic water annihilating her limbs. The sea was for ever. Nothing of men and women, of humankind, ever was.

'Here we are, then,' Andy said, hacking up a gobbet of phlegm and spitting it into the water as the engine cut out and he steered the boat towards a jetty. It looked like a child's drawing, Beth thought, a few bars of wood thrown together by an unpractised hand.

'Watch how you go,' Andy said, as Hamish bashed his shin on the anchor while making his way towards the prow.

He dismissed the offer of Andy's lobster-red hand and lunged on to the jetty's slimy surface. 'Shit!'

'Said 'twas slippery.' Unvarnished delight glinted for a moment over the entrenched resentment. Hamish decided that he detested Andy and would not tip him for the ride.

But Beth was already fishing out a fiver from her purse. 'Lift's part of the cottage rental,' Andy said, trousering the note. 'Take the bags up, will I?' He began manhandling the two suitcases and the assorted bags on to a rusting supermarket trolley.

'For Christ's sake, watch it!' Hamish shouted as his case toppled over, and simultaneously Beth called out, 'Don't worry!' Andy rescued the case, spat, rubbed in the seagull droppings with his sleeve and began to push the trolley determinedly up a track that ran through waves of mauve and pink and purple.

Beth and Hamish followed him. The rutted track went steeply upwards and then ran along the cliff top. Below them, massive breakers were thrashing the rocks for dear life. A butterfly made a crazy chalk-blue zigzag across the heather.

'I'm happy,' Beth called back over her shoulder.

Tough heather stalks were assaulting Hamish's ankles. His socks provided no protection from the midges. Already he could feel a blister forming where his left shoe pinched. They reached a solitary white-painted cottage, where Andy pushed open the door, trundled in the trolley and proceeded to dump the contents on to the floor. 'There you are, then.' He made as if to walk off.

'What about heat, light and so on?' Hamish asked.

'S'all over there on the notice. Heating's Calor, spare's under the sink. Firewood and coal's in the shed round the back. Ferry goes once a day, 'cept Thursdays. If you need to shop other times, give us a ring. Me mobile's on top of the notice. Me dad don't have one but his phone's on the notice too. Ta-ta for now.'

'I brought our leftovers. We can have the cold sausages and I'll do some potatoes. It's nice, isn't it?' Beth asked, willing herself, unsuccessfully, not to plead.

Hamish was staring out of the kitchen window. 'It feels damp.'

'A fire'll soon change that.'

'It'll take more than a fire to cure this.'

'But the view's fabulous.'

'If you like unrelieved vistas of ocean.'

'Are you going to find nothing but fault with the house as well as with me?' Beth asked.

She walked into the bedroom and began to make up the bed. The sheets were damp. Hamish was right. Her head began to fill with the familiar maggots of despair. 'What is the point?' she asked herself aloud. 'Nothing's right.' And nothing will ever make it right, the maggots voicelessly murmured. She looked about for a hot-water bottle and found one in the bathroom. Mentally, she held the warm perished rubber to her belly, vainly hoping to keep the maggots at bay.

'I'll put a bottle in the bed to take the chill off,' she said, sounding to herself like her own mother. 'Look, there're games here,' she said, pulling out a drawer of the dresser. 'Scrabble and chess and so on.'

'I hate board games. Have you brought the antihistamine cream? I'm being eaten alive by these bloody midges.'

Beth, who always packed antihistamine, Lomotil, paracetamol, TCP and Savlon, against Hamish's hypochondria, said, 'Damn. It was that row about your mother. I forgot to pack it.'

'Shit.'

'Why don't you bring your own bloody antihistamine? It's you who gets bitten. I'm going for a walk.'

The path stretched beyond the cottage along the cliff top. A little way along, Beth stopped to examine a vertiginous track down to the cove below. A patch of gleaming sand was appearing beneath the irregular recession of glass-green and milk-white waves. Beth thought, He might push me over right here and I wouldn't care.

'We could swim there tomorrow,' she said, as Hamish caught her up.

'Too rough.' The waves were punishing the rocks with professional violence. Scotland had been Beth's idea. Hamish had a hunch that she had tried to reach him through sentiment for his Scottish father – his father lost so long ago that he was at best a regret for an absence of feeling.

Beth said, 'I'll go back and put the potatoes on.'

'I'll walk on a bit if that's okay.'

What if it isn't? Beth thought.

The cottage, as she arrived at the door, looked bleak,

its whitewash rusty and discoloured. The pale blue window frames, flaking from the assault of wind and brine, put her in mind of Andy's sleep-caked eyes. The prospect of the coming evening with Hamish was alarming. Almost she welcomed his mother's pending presence.

Hamish was up early to be at the airport. He rang Nicky, aware that it was partly to get it over with.

'Hi.'

'Hi.'

When did we start saying 'Hi'? he wondered. Was it the war?

'You okay, Nick?'

'Not really.'

'Oh, why?' Hamish saw Andy's contemptuous smile.

'I miss you.'

'Miss you too, babe.'

'Hurry back.'

'I'll do my best.' Though that is never quite good enough for women, he reflected.

The arrival of his mother's plane was announced as 'On time' and against his own wishes he began to feel excitement. It was seven, no, eight years since he had seen her. Only phone calls at Christmas hung between that last meeting, like paper lanterns at a garden party, whose 'light' is purely theoretical. She never rang on his birthday. He doubted she remembered it. Very likely, she had chosen to forget it, eliminating her only child's birthday as a way of ablating her own.

She must be nearly fifty. Beth, when she had first met his mother, said that she looked like his elder sister. But they were polite, both of them, the two women in his life. When they had met last, when he and Beth had stopped on their way back from the Italian lakes and spent the night in Zurich, the two women had performed together as if expertly choreographed, what was unspoken between them creating its own strange bond.

A hand touched his shoulder so lightly that he jumped.

'Darling.'

'Mother.'

'"Mother", darling?' The humorous note deputized for reproach.

'Sorry. It's been a long time.'

He looked at his mother's face, trying to find, as he always did on their rare reunions, some clue to the consuming hopelessness she kindled in him. Tall, her hair still its natural colour, naturally blonde, with a few silver threads co-mingling with the gold, in khaki trousers hugging hipbones a teenager would have been proud of, a little silk cardigan slung over narrow shoulders, she still looked – what? He was uneasily aware that had she not been his mother he might have found her desirable.

'Is this all your luggage?' He could not yet quite bring

himself to use the name she had insisted on when he was a small child. 'Una, darling, not "Mum", please.'

'I always travel light. I take all my luggage as "hand".'

Her case was light too: a chic Swiss affair with super-efficient wheels. Really, she should be running some multinational company. 'You should be running ICI or something.'

'Darling, you are sweet.'

He'd forgotten her knack for turning even an intentional insult into a clever compliment.

As he started the car, his mobile rang. 'Has she landed?'

Covering the phone, he said, falsely genial, 'All safe and sound.'

'How is she?'

'Fine.'

'We forgot to bring any wine. Can you buy some?'

He wanted to say, Are you drinking already? But said instead, 'How much shall I get?'

'Enough to drown her in preferably. and then me,' Beth said, and rang off.

'That was Beth.' It was probably only in his imagination that his mother's expression became amused. Her natural set of her mouth was a faint, cat-like smile.

'How is Beth, darling?'

'Beth's good.' Beth *is* good, he thought and felt a pang.

'I'm longing to see her.' Una lit a cigarette. 'It's sweet of you both to ask me to stay.'

We didn't ask you, Hamish thought. 'Una, would you mind, only Beth doesn't like smoke in the car.'

His mother opened the window, made as if to throw her cigarette out and then said, 'But I mustn't start a fire. Where would you like me to put it, darling?'

'Oh, finish it, it doesn't matter – I can open the windows to air the car.'

They drove in silence. The outskirts of Glasgow gave way to lowlands, which in turn gave place to rolling heights, swathed in muted purple and russet and green. Coming to the gleaming edge of Loch Lomond, his mother said, 'I hope they never find it.'

Irritated that he knew what she was referring to, Hamish feigned obtuseness. 'Find what?'

'I imagine the monster having some terribly deep lair. Don't you wish you had one, darling?'

He didn't feel like explaining that she had confused the lochs. 'Would you like some music? This is the latest by a new client of mine. Leo Jones.' The lead singer of the band 'Pard' had commissioned Hamish as architect to redo his new house. It was a big contract and, with Nicky's tastes to cater for, as well as a mortgage, he needed it.

'Darling, how marvellous.'

It was unclear whether she meant the job or the music, but 'Pard' saw them through another fifty miles while Una slept.

She looked older sleeping. She must dread growing

old. Hamish wished he could reassure her that it was not the face and figure which counted but the personality, the heart. But that wasn't so. Or it hadn't been so for him and Beth.

'*You take the high road and I'll take the low road,*' said his mother, waking suddenly.

Hamish braked sharply, mistaking this for an instruction. Behind them, a lorry's hooter bellowed a warning.

'*For me and my true love will never meet again / On the bonny, bonny banks of Loch Lomond,*' Una continued, singing now. Her voice was a fine contralto, unforced. 'Of course it wasn't Ness at all. I was muddling the lochs. Silly of me.' Hamish was disarmed further when she added, 'Your father sang that to me the night he died. I say "sang", though he could hardly speak, poor lamb. But I heard the words.'

'He was conscious?'

'In and out. I came here with him, you know?'

'Where?'

'Quite near here.'

'But where near?' Not, please God, Hamish prayed, to the island. His mother had always had a touch of the uncanny about her.

'Loch Fyne. They smoke fish wonderfully. We stayed in a tiny hotel with the sweetest people running it. Our bed was diabolically soft and the bath water was brown as mud. Alastair was terribly worried about it, but I told him it would be wonderful for the skin. It's the peat.'

'What?'

'The brown.'

'Oh, yes,' Hamish said. A fugitive image of his father dissolved into a memory of Beth on their wedding night standing by a faux-Victorian bath, with taps shaped as swans, crying. 'Yes,' he said again. 'The water in the cottage here is brown.'

'Terrifically good for our skins, darling.'

As they crossed the old bridge, his mother lit another cigarette. Hamish hesitated, then left this unremarked. It was not far now to the head of the island. The ferry would have left and Andy would, if he had followed instructions, be waiting. Hamish thought: I could knock him down and drive the car straight into the harbour. I wonder how long we'd float before we'd drown?

'Almost there,' he said cheerily.

Andy was polite in Una's company. She offered him a cigarette, which he accepted with an almost civil expression of gratitude. He took them across the strait at full lick and dropped them at the landing-stage, promising to return the following morning for any 'errands'. Hamish, who suspected this was nosiness rather than any desire to help, rejected the offer, but Andy repeated that he would be 'passing anyway' so he 'might as well'.

'Where do you live, Andy?' His mother's voice sounded authentically interested.

'Round that cove, there.' He waved a casual lobster

hand. 'Me and me brother lives there. Me dad lives up by the hermit's.'

'A hermit? Hamish, darling, how exciting. I've always had a faint yen to become a hermit.'

But Andy had started the motor and was maniacally roaring away, either deafened by the boat's engine or pretending not to hear.

Beth met them at the door, wearing a blue apron covered in ancient bleach spots, which she'd found, she said, hanging in a cupboard in the kitchen. Hamish's suspicions that this was part of some play act were confirmed when she produced macaroni cheese, followed by apple crumble.

Una, with cries of 'How lovely, darling!', pushed the macaroni around the plate, ate two pieces of tomato and made a few dabs at the apple smouldering beneath molten crumble.

'Would you like some custard, Una? Bird's best.' Beth was apparently enjoying playing the part of a substandard cook.

'Darling, it was delicious. May I look round?' Una had gone into their bedroom without waiting for an answer.

'Charming,' she called to them. 'Clever things. You *have* done well finding this.'

Beth, coming into the room behind her, said, 'You can hear the sea at night.' She had heard it flailing against the impervious rocks, out of time with her own surging heart.

I hate you, I hate you, Una, she thought. It's you have made him like this, cowed and cowardly. Aloud she said, 'If you lean out and twist your head, you can see the sea down to the right.'

'*We joined the navy to see the world / And what did we see? We saw the sea,*' Hamish sang jauntily, joining them. He pushed open the stiff metal-framed window for Una, who leant out. 'You can almost smell the air doing you good,' he suggested.

'What you whispering for?' Nicky wanted to know.

'My mother's here.'

'What, there now?'

'I'm just going out!' Hamish called to a solitary sheep, his hand over the phone. He was crouched, leeward of the wind, behind a rock.

Nicky giggled, encouraged by this apparent display of recklessness. 'What's she like, your mum?'

'Oh, I don't know, she's my mother.'

'Does she look like you?'

'I'm supposed to look like my father.'

'Short and dark and hairy?'

'Thanks for the vote of appreciation.'

'Little men are sexier,' said Nicky. From her success in ruffling him, she knew she had recovered ground. 'They have more testosterone. It's a scientific fact. I read it in one of the Sundays. When you coming back?'

'I don't know,' Hamish said. 'If you ring me with

THE BOY WHO COULD SEE DEATH

some crisis about the house, I can probably swing it to come. What's the news there anyway?'

When he returned to the cottage, Beth was on her knees trying to light a fire. Seeing her kneeling on the bit of tatty old carpet on the stone floor, patiently feeding the fire-lighter's faint blue flame, he felt compunction. He bustled about making a business of collecting wood and coal from the shed, wondering how they were going to fill the time.

His mother lay on the sofa, reading. He envied her tranquillity, the effortless way she ignored the trivia of everyday life. Was it that she had always been pampered, or that she had been pampered because her character enlisted the unquestioned support of any environment in which she found herself?

'What are you reading, Una?'

'*Kidnapped.*'

If she had said, 'Kierkegaard' he would have been less surprised. 'I wouldn't have reckoned on you as a boys' adventure girl.'

'I'm reading all Stevenson. Your father used to read him aloud to me.'

'Really?' She could easily be making this up. You could never tell with Una. God knew what story she was going to weave about Stefan, now his earthly presence had finally been removed and with it any corresponding constraints on the truth.

Beth said, 'Hamish, did you get the wine?'

'Hell, I forgot. And the antihistamine.'

Later that night, Beth rolled cautiously towards Hamish down the pitched mattress.

'Not with her next door, Bethy. The walls are very thin.'

They both lay assuming sleep, aware of the vast chasm that opens so easily between the closest physical proximities.

When Beth woke next morning, the sun was spinning a tissue of light through the curtain and on to the glass-topped dressing table. Fragments of sunbeam winked and quavered as the curtain filled in the mild breeze. Beside her, Hamish, in his tartan nightshirt, his cheeks pink and soft with sleep, resembled a big bristly baby. Observing his pillowed face, she felt none of the usual knives of hatred: no emotion, no passion, no nostalgia. Nothing. How could you feel nothing? She might have had a cardiac lobotomy for all the feeling in her heart.

She eased her hips out of bed, and moved quietly across the room. Una was already in the kitchen, lighting the stove amid the sinister anaesthetic smell of Calor gas. It looked as if she had nothing on under her towelling dressing gown.

'Were you warm enough, Una?'

'Snug as a bug, darling.'

'There are more blankets in our wardrobe.'

Una made a dismissive gesture. Beth noticed that

she had shed the diamond rings she had arrived with and was now wearing only a plain platinum band. The hands were Hamish's – long and brown with clean, well-manicured nails. 'More blankets and I'd suffocate. I'm putting this on for tea but I'm going for a swim first.'

'Really?'

'Come too?'

'I don't want to disturb Hamish. My costume's in the bedroom,' Beth said, not at all wanting to swim.

'Don't wear one. I'm not.' Una exposed a polished brown shoulder.

'Oh,' Beth said. She didn't want to appear prudish but swimming naked! Scotland wasn't the South of France. Trust Una. Why did she have to be so *different?*

'There's no one to see,' Una said, reading her thoughts.

'Maybe another time,' Beth said. 'I'll make the tea so it's ready when you get back. You'll need it.' And, 'Be careful,' she couldn't help calling out. 'The path down to the cove looks treacherously steep.'

'Who are you shouting at?'

'Your mother,' Beth said. 'She's gone off to swim stark naked.'

'She always did swim naked if she could,' he recalled.

'It's showing off. This isn't St Tropez. What'll the natives think?'

'*What'll the neighbours say?*'

Hamish had once played Dai Bread in a production of *Under Milk Wood* at university. He trotted out this tired old quote, Beth thought, whenever he wanted to suggest she was being conventional.

'I don't give a monkey's about nudity, as you know. We're visitors and it's just not good manners. I happen to think manners matter.'

'Is the kettle boiling dry for any special reason?'

They were drinking tea in silence when Una returned, her hair like seaweed, her keen-boned, ship's-figurehead face flushed from the cold.

'It was heavenly,' she said, 'the water.'

Beth, doubting this, said, 'There's tea in the pot.'

'Darling,' Una said, 'how lovely. I'll have a bath first, if I may?'

'Now she's taking all the hot water,' Beth said, as they heard water run into the bath.

The phone rang, making them both jump, and Hamish answered quickly, assuming a breezy tone.

'Hello there.'

'Morning, squire. I'm off over to Seil. Want anything?'

'Oh, Andy. Good morning.' Hamish made a face at Beth. 'Do we want anything?' he asked, covering the phone.

'Drink,' Beth said. 'Lashings of it.'

'You talk to him.'

Beth took the phone and said, 'Good morning, Andy. Yes, thank you, we're fine. It would be good if you could bring . . . oh? Well, that's very kind. Yes, thank you, I'd like to. When should I be there?'

'I'm going with him,' she said blithely to Hamish. 'He's picking me up at the landing-stage.'

'There was no need for that.'

'I know there wasn't,' Beth said. 'I thought you might like some time by yourself —'

As she was leaving, his phone signalled the arrival of a text. 'Better get that,' Beth said. 'Might be your assistant about your new project.' Her eyes showed the ironical gleam he hated. 'I'll let you know when I'm on the way back.'

In her Fair Isle jersey, she looked pitifully young. Hamish had a sudden urge to yell something nice after her but could only think of 'Hey, remember antihistamine.'

'Darling,' said Una. 'Do stop fretting. I'm fine.'

It wasn't his mother he was fretting over. Nicky had texted that she would call him in ten minutes. While he could have managed, just about, a dialogue with Nick in front of Beth, a coded conversation in the presence of his mother was impossible. She had, he remembered all too uncomfortably from childhood, a code-breaker's mind.

'All right if I go for a saunter?' he asked.

Una didn't bother to answer. She was apparently lost in Robert Louis Stevenson.

Hamish walked along the cliff top. The wind hurtling off the sea made his nose run. However could his mother

bathe in this temperature? Beth was right. It was showing off. He took the phone from his pocket and inspected
it for missed calls. Nothing. He walked on past a cluster
of sheep which stood staring after him with mild, incurious faces.

At the head of the bluff, he was about to turn to
retrace his steps when he saw a figure just below where
the path dipped, and then branched inland. It was a
woman wearing what at first looked like a long grey
cloak, but, on moving closer, Hamish saw that it was a
blanket. It had red stitching round its hem, like the old
hospital blankets, and was fastened below her neck with
a large safety pin, giving the woman the appearance of
some ancient warrior queen of legend.

'Hi.' In the light of this impression, the greeting was
unexpected. Her voice was soft and youthful, though
she looked well over middle age. 'I'm Pegotty.'

'Hi, I'm Hamish.'

'I'm the hermit,' the woman said. 'Perhaps they've
told you.'

Hamish was spared the puzzle of how to reply to this
by the bass buzzing of the phone in his pocket. The
woman gave him a magisterial nod and walked on.

'Hi, Nick.'

'Where are you?'

'Out. I went for a walk.'

'Escaping her?'

'Beth's not here. It was my mother I was escaping.'

'Oh,' Nicky said. She sounded regretful that it was not his wife he needed to flee from.

'I've just met a hermit,' he said, for something to say.

'What's he doing there?'

'It's a she,' Hamish said.

'You're joking!'

'No. She introduced herself.'

'What's she called?'

'I don't know,' Hamish said. He didn't feel like going into the hermit's odd name.

'Probably sex starved. Bet she'll try to get her leg over.'

'She's sixty if she's a day. She looks like Old Mother Hubbard. She was wearing a blanket.'

'An old hippy.'

'Probably.' The hermit, who he had hoped might be a diversion, was proving to be an impediment. 'How's the builder?'

'Not here. No one's here but me.'

'Fuck!'

'I wish.'

'You'd better ring him.'

'You ring him,' Nicky said. 'I'm just the assistant. It's the boss has to kick arse.'

The builder explained that his wife's hip was bad and he was having to mind the kids while she lay down. He was going to send Kevin over later that day with a gang of men to start the job off. They would like Kevin, he assured Hamish. Kevin was reliable. (Here Hamish had to stifle the suggestion that what was conveyed by this was that the builder himself wasn't.) The builder himself would look in tomorrow, always providing the hip wasn't still giving the wife gyp, in which case he'd have to run her over to the doctor's.

Hamish rang Nicky back. 'His wife's done something to her leg so he's having to mind the children. He's sending someone over later today.'

'How late? I don't believe it anyway. What's the matter with her leg?'

'I don't know,' said Hamish. 'Actually, it's her hip.'

'You said leg.'

'I'll ring him and ask him to ring your mobile when this other man is on his way.'

'I don't want to be here all day.'

'No,' said Hamish. 'I'll tell him to call. The other man's name is Kevin, by the way.'

He was coming down a steep drop, thinking that this must be as good for the hamstrings as the gym, when he almost ran into the hermit. She was sitting on the phone-booth rock, looking out to sea. Hamish, not knowing what the etiquette with hermits was, wondered if he should walk by. But she gave a welcoming smile.

'It's all right. It's only other people's houses I don't go into.'

'I wasn't sure. I've not met a . . . er, before.'

'Not many have. We're thin on the ground. Like a Polo?' She offered him a stub of green-and-silver paper.

'Thanks.' Hamish, who disliked mint, but didn't want to seem churlish, took one.

'You must be holidaying here.'

'Yes. With my wife. And my mother.' He had a sudden awkward vision of the hermit meeting Una and mistaking her for his wife.

The hermit pulled a far from pious face. 'Brave man. Or perhaps you like your mother?'

'Not really,' said Hamish, feeling the pleasure and remorse of honest confession. 'But my stepfather's just died so –'

'She parked herself on you?'

'I guess.'

'I long ago decided that guilt is nature's way of preventing us from killing our parents. I can't see the evolutionary point of it otherwise. Of course, Freud would say that the causal link is the other way round. A reaction to the wish to bump them off. I disagree.' She spoke with a careful diction, as if she were delivering a lesson to deaf children.

'I haven't really thought about it,' Hamish said. It wasn't the sort of conversation he was used to.

The hermit explained: 'I was a psychologist once.'

'Oh.'

'I can't help thinking about people when I meet them. It's why I have to live alone. To stop myself.'

'Does it work?'

'Sometimes,' the hermit said, leaning forward to rub her shins. She pushed herself up stiffly from her rocky base. Under some mud-stained black trousers, she had on odd-coloured socks, one grey wool, one electric-blue. Her eyes, which were not quite true, were a strange mix of blue and hazel. 'I've got slightly better at it over the years.' She looked at Hamish with her orthogonal eyes. 'I'll see you around.'

Beth felt the cleansing breeze of a reclaimed freedom as Andy raced the boat at full tilt across the strait. She didn't mind a bit that he was speeding in order to impress her. Hamish had taken a dislike to Andy, so she had decided that she would get along with him.

'Been married long?' he shouted suddenly.

'What?' Beth's eyes were busy patrolling the dark grey water for seals.

'You and hubby. Been together long?'

'Seven years,' Beth shouted back into the roar.

'No kids?'

'Not so far.'

'Be coming up to the seven-year itch, then,' Andy suggested, squinting into the sun with an undisguised leer.

Hamish, on the rock which the hermit had vacated, was fielding calls like flung stones. Kevin had not arrived or rung, the builder was not answering his phone and as far as Nicky was concerned the whole lot of them could go and fuck themselves. She had cut her phone off just as a shadow fell on to the path, and looking up he saw the enigmatic face of his mother.

She smiled down, detached and inquiring, and he said, angry at having to explain himself at all, 'This bloody job. Trying to sort it from here is driving me mad.'

'Poor darling,' said his mother. She continued to look down on him with her ambiguous little half-smile. She was wearing a thin black nylon jacket of a type that only the unsophisticated would imagine inexpensive.

'It's my job,' he said, as if answering a reproach. 'I'm the architect and he's paying me handsomely. Very. I'm going to have to go back down to London to see to this mess. It's urgent, but Beth won't understand.'

'Poor lamb,' said Una. 'What a bore.'

Hamish had a terrible apprehension that at any moment he might begin to cry. 'I don't think Beth's got any idea how tough it is out there.' He knew this to be untrue. Beth, while concerned to protect her holiday, was soberly worldly-wise.

His mother, still looking down on him, put out her hand, a gesture which produced an instinctive recoil, though, so far as he could remember, she had never hit him. The hand landed gently on the crown of his head, as if it were conferring an honour or a blessing. 'Poor lamb,' she repeated. 'Shall we walk?'

They walked, his mother ahead, in single file along the cliff top. Sea pinks and strange succulents poked out at right angles down the steep cliff-face to the ragged, foaming edges of the sea. On their other side, thrush-egg harebells threaded the stiff grass. Some shorn, ascetic-looking sheep stopped munching apparently to observe their passage and then resumed their ruminations. A phrase of song drifted to his ears over his mother's back. '*Mary, my Scots bluebell.*' She called out to him, 'Did you know it's the harebell, darling?'

'What?' Hamish shouted back. An untreated childhood illness had left him slightly deaf in one ear. Another reason to hate her.

'The bluebell, darling,' said his mother, confusingly.

They had reached the point where the path descended to a fork, the place where Hamish had first met the hermit. He hoped she might show up again now. Walking behind his mother had brought back the miserable anxiety of trotting behind her as a boy. He was always, on his holiday visits to his stepfather's luxurious and empty Zurich home, supposing he had lost her: in department stores, in parks, in car parks. Once, in the house, he had run frantically from room to room looking for her, and had found her at last, smelling of talcum powder, coming out of the bathroom wrapped in nothing but a white towel. 'Silly darling,' she had

said, when he explained why he was crying. 'Not "lost",
just mislaid.'

Hamish had rung Beth. 'I'm going to have to stay down
here a bit.'

'Oh?'

'Leo's making sounds like he's pulling out.'

'Oh. Whatever you have to do.'

'Beth. I need this. There's slim pickings out there
these days. And we have an overdraft.'

'We?'

'I do. The business does.'

'I know that,' Beth had said. 'D'you want to talk to
your mother?'

'Not particularly. Is she behaving?'

'She's fine,' Beth said, and rang off.

'You dealt with the wife, then?' Nicky asked.

Not liking this turn of phrase, Hamish returned it
sharply. 'Yes, I've "dealt" with her.'

'No need to take that tone.'

'What tone?'

'That "don't speak like that about my precious wife"
tone. If you feel like that about her, why are you fucking
me?'

Good question, Hamish thought, but aloud said, 'For
God's sake, Nick, please. I'm worried about the Leo
project.'

'D'you think he's really going to pull out?'

'It's possible. You know these guys, they're flighty.'

'We'd better get on to him, then.'

Leo was unaccountably 'tied up' over the next few days. Hamish went through a couple of other possible projects, none as lucrative or as likely to attract future custom. Nicky was not reassuring. She made much of Leo's failure to return calls and was sexually demanding.

One evening, out to dinner, when he should have been enjoying their relative freedom from Beth's proximity, Hamish received a text.

'Shit!'

'What?'

'Look at that!'

Nicky read out, as if to the restaurant at large, '*hi, sorry to keep missing you. plans changed. accountant wants me to relocate to ireland. gr8 knowing you and thanx 4 yr help. send yr invoice to martin. cheers leo.*'

'Well, I did say.'

'What did you say?'

'I said it was mad to go away when you did.'

'Oh, great. Thanks Nicky.'

'You're welcome.'

Paying the bill, he said, 'Look, I need to go back to the house tonight.'

'Sure, I'll come too.'

'No, Nick. I can't have you at the house.'

'Worried what the neighbours'll say?'

'No. Not really. It's Beth's house too.'

'Oh, yeah, I get it. Running home to Mummy?'

'Beth's not my mother.'

'You sure?'

But maybe she was right, Hamish thought, lying sleepless in the comfortable matrimonial bed. Beth's pyjama bottoms were still under her pillow. They smelt reassuringly of her herbal bath stuff. Sweet but not too sweet. Natural. She was natural. And naturally kind. Very kind.

Later that night, when sleep was still avoiding him, in the small hours, when even those with tunnel vision may see over their shoulders, he got up and made himself a cup of Beth's herbal tea. He had been in the habit of mocking her for these. 'Teasing', he had called it when she had rounded on him. 'Only teasing. Where's your sense of humour?' 'You know what?' she'd snapped back. 'That's what all sadists say. "Only teasing."'

Was he a sadist? Maybe he was. Maybe he attacked Beth because she was maternal. Because she provided what his mother never had.

On an impulse he rang Beth but her phone was switched off. A wave of shocking loneliness swept through him and he hugged the pyjamas closer. Dear Beth. He almost wept thinking of how kind she had been to him over the years. She had stuck by him faithfully and he had treated her shabbily. He missed her. He would 'deal with' Nicky and make it up to Beth. Tomorrow he would go back to their holiday. Take her for walks. Make love to her. With Beth there even the thought of his mother seemed a comforting prospect.

Andy met Hamish with the boat.

'Been having fun in London, then?'

'It was work, actually.' His foot nudged a cigarette end. Lipstick stained.

It had been work. Too nervous to call Nicky to announce his departure, he had texted her with vague words about seeing her on his return and she had responded with predictable venom.

'How long you been gone, then?' Andy was revving up the motor with his customary violence.

'Just over a week.' More cigarette ends, red from his mother's smiling lips.

'More like ten days.'

'Nine, actually.'

It was possible Nicky might pull some stunt. A 'suicide'. She had half threatened it once before. Or, worse, tell Beth. Hatred swept over him as he contemplated this. If she did fucking well attempt suicide he could only pray she succeeded.

'Girls been having fun on their own, I reckon.'

'I hope so.' Not too likely. Poor Beth. Stuck with his

mother. He would enjoy making it up to her. If only he'd thought to bring her a present. He'd given Nicky so many gifts and grudged Beth even her simple wish to buy new curtains for the bedroom.

Andy winked a canny, red-rimmed eye and nodded at his binoculars. 'Reckon they have. While the cat's away, yeah . . .?'

The cottage, when Hamish reached it – breathing hard with his excitement of getting back and his eagerness to be reunited with Beth – was empty. On the table in the kitchen was his mother's copy of *Kidnapped* and beside it a chessboard apparently left mid-game.

He remembered now that his mother had tried to teach him one summer, but he had been too nervous of misunderstanding the rules to learn properly. She had abandoned the attempt with 'Never mind, darling, you haven't got a chess mind. Not everyone has.'

But Beth, did she play chess? Not to his knowledge. Never with him, certainly.

He looked into the bedroom. Both beds were neatly made. The house seemed too quiet. The tidy kitchen, the washed crockery on the draining board and the vase of wild flowers on the mantelpiece offered no clue to the whereabouts of any occupants.

A little way along the cliff path he saw the hermit ahead of him. He called out a greeting and she turned and waved cheerily and yelled back something incomprehensible.

He quickened his pace, meaning to catch up with her, for, suddenly, he felt in need of a friendly soul, but she disappeared over a heathery mound.

Hamish turned back along the cliff in time to see his wife and his mother emerge from the track that led down to the sea. They were both wrapped in towels, so it would have been hard to say quite why it was obvious to him that beneath the towels they were naked.

'Darling, how nice. Beth and I have been for our swim.'

Hamish stared at Beth. 'You don't like swimming.'

'Oh, I don't know,' his wife said, and she looked at him, as later he was to reconstruct the scene, with an expression on her face that he had never met before. 'Una and I have been swimming together, quite a lot, in fact, since you left us. I like it now. Don't I, Una?'

'Yes, darling,' said his mother, and she laid a slender brown hand lightly, but proprietarily, on Beth's white forearm.

Something old and hard and deeply buried within him began to sound warning signals. 'But you don't like swimming,' he said again, staring at his wife, who stared back calmly as the ancient tears of childhood welled treacherously in his eyes.

'She does now.'

His mother was looking at Beth and smiling a smile which, he was later to see, was only one of a long chain of smiles that had, oh so finely and deftly, wrought his exclusion.

'Beth?' There was a horrible note of appeal in his voice. An appeal that, even as he heard it, he knew had the ring of a lost cause.

'Tastes change, darling,' his mother said, turning from her son back to her son's wife with her mysterious little half-smile.

Read on to discover the exclusive opening chapter of *Cousins*, the next compelling novel from Salley Vickers . . .

Cousins

When a persistent ringing startled me from a sleep of unusual contentment I swear I knew it was about Will. I'm not blessed with second sight but my intuition has always been sharp. Or maybe it was simply that Will was the person in our family most likely to be the source of a late night phone call.

Or early morning I should say. For when I woke up properly, and found that the recovery of the shoes I lost on my sixth birthday – they were blue-spotted and I never found their like again – was a cruel illusion, I saw from my bedside clock that it was 2 a.m. The clock was the Babar clock which my cousin Cecilia had brought me from Paris. The end of Babar's trunk moves up and down as the clock ticks, which could sound annoying but I loved it. I found the ticking soothing and have it by my bed still.

The phone had stopped ringing and had started again by the time my father got to it. I could hear him in the hall below sounding apprehensive and annoyed. And then I heard his voice change and become urgent.

He was calling my mother, who joined him in the hall, and hearing the tone of their voices I got up and went halfway downstairs and sat on the landing, which is where I used to sit when eavesdropping.

Through the stair rails I could partly see my parents in their pyjamas. My father was holding my mother, who was crying. She rarely cried so I knew this was serious.

I waited a little on the landing but the worry of not knowing what had happened was too great so I ran down the remaining stairs.

'Hetta!'

'Dad, what is it?'

I was right, it was Will. At first I thought he must be dead but it turned out to be worse than that.

At the time I was immersed in the Brontës and saw myself as Emily, wild and poetical and in love with her brother. And while Will and I were never close (I was too much his younger sister for that) he did have some of Branwell Brontë's qualities. And weaknesses.

It's hard to say how far I felt the gravity of what had happened as a real event, which was to alter all our lives, rather than a drama in my Brontë persona. All I understood then was that Will was in hospital and that both my parents were to go at once and that, as I could not be left alone indefinitely, and there was no one obvious to call upon to come to the house to keep me company, I was to drive with them to Cambridge.

We left there and then and I have always supposed that we were all still in our pyjamas but reviewing everything now I can see that was unlikely. Maybe just I was. I certainly slept in the back of the car and woke to hear my parents talking in the voices people use when they don't want to be overheard.

My father was saying, and there was a terrifying note of despair in his voice, 'It's Nathaniel all over again.'

I know I heard this and it isn't the construction of hindsight because my Uncle Nathaniel was hardly ever mentioned and his name had a special allure for me. He was my father's elder brother and was killed in a climbing accident, the kind of event which my tragic imagination relished. I had written some poems in my Emily Brontë mode for my dead uncle, one of which began:

> *Oh you who are lost to us, still you are with us,*
> *Lost in the flesh but held in the heart,*
> *Still we shall mourn for you, though we are silent,*
> *Dumb though we be we are never apart.*

As far as I remember it went on in a similar vein and I doubt it improved.

I don't recall what my mother said to my father's anguished comment but maybe for the first time I had some sense of what the death of my uncle might have meant to his family and it was fear that made me exclaim, 'Will's not dead, is he?'

My mother was more level-headed than my father, who had a fair measure of his family's emotional lability, and she would certainly have tried to soothe my fears. But anxiety had been awoken, a real and not a dramatic anxiety, and I was no longer consumptive Emily Brontë with a poetical tempest raging in my breast but robustly, indecently hale, fifteen-year-old Henrietta Tye, whose brother Will, it seemed, had suffered some appalling injury.